Alice
ON THE OUTSIDE

Books by Phyllis Reynolds Naylor

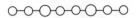

Alice
ON THE OUTSIDE

Phyllis

Reynolds

Naylor

A Jean Karl Book

Atheneum Books for Young Readers

For Isabelle Archibald

Atheneum Books for Young Readers
An imprint of Simon & Schuster
Children's Publishing Division
1230 Avenue of the Americas
New York, New York 10020

Book design by Nina Barnett
The text of this book is set in Berkeley Oldstyle
Printed in the United States of America
10 9 8 7 6 5 4 3

Library of Congress Cataloging-in-Publication Data
Naylor, Phyllis Reynolds.
Alice on the outside / Phyllis Reynolds Naylor.—1st ed.
p. cm.
"A Jean Karl book."
Summary: Eighth-grader Alice has lots of questions about sex, relation-
ships, prejudice, and change.
ISBN 0-689-80359-1
[1. Interpersonal relations—Fiction. 2. Sex—Fiction. 3. Prejudices—
Fiction. 4. Single-parent families—Fiction. 5. Schools—Fiction.] I. Title.
PS7.N24Ald   1999
[Fic]—dc21   98-7992

FIRST
EDITION

CONTENTS

Teasing Sal

Dad says it's the dumbest thing he ever saw, but every year the *Washington Post* comes out with a list of what's "in" and what's "out"—movies, songs, food, clothes, TV programs, even people. It's done sort of tongue in cheek, but I read it anyway.

"Al," he says (he and Lester call me Al), "are you really going to let somebody else tell you what you should be eating and wearing and talking about? You're not a zombie, remember. You're an interesting girl with a brain of her own."

I like my dad. I know kids who are always knocking their parents, but Dad manages to squeeze in a compliment even when he's trying to teach me a lesson. I know if Mom were alive I'd love her too, but she died when I was in kindergarten.

"Imagine waking up some morning and finding

out that everything in your closet and refrigerator was on the 'out' list," said Pamela, when we were discussing the list. She and Elizabeth are two of my very best friends.

"Imagine waking up and finding your *name* on the 'out' list," I said. "One day you're part of the 'in' crowd, and the next you're not."

"Then they weren't real friends to begin with," said Elizabeth.

We were walking home from the library, enjoying the first faint feel of spring, a warm breeze that ruffled our hair. We were ready for spring—ready for something new. Elizabeth had a new boyfriend, Justin Collier, the absolutely handsomest guy in eighth grade. Elizabeth was the first one of us who had been invited to the eighth-grade semi-formal in May.

Pamela had already turned fourteen, and she was ready for anything too, especially anything that would take her away from the mess at home—namely, her mom's running off to be with her NordicTrack instructor.

As for me, it was time to concentrate on where my own life was going. Miss Summers, my gorgeous seventh-grade English teacher whom my dad loves, is going to England for a year as an exchange teacher because she can't decide between Dad and our assistant principal, Jim

Sorringer, who's in love with her too. After worrying about my dad's love life for over a year, I decided it was out of my hands and I wasn't going to waste any more of my life trying to work things out for him.

"Bring on the spring!" I said, lifting my face toward the sun and feeling it full on my cheeks and forehead. "Gwen says you can be a candy striper at the hospital once you're fourteen. That's what she's going to do this summer."

"Who's Gwen?" asked Pamela.

"The short black girl in my math class."

"Do they pay you?" she wanted to know.

"I don't think so. It's all volunteer."

"I won't be fourteen till December," said Elizabeth. "I guess that leaves me out."

"I'm not volunteering at any hospital! Who wants to empty bedpans all day?" said Pamela.

"I think candy stripers deliver magazines and mail and stuff," I told her. But I could tell it still didn't appeal much. Pamela was depressed enough without working in a hospital. Was it possible we'd each be doing something different come summer? It would be the first time since we'd known each other that we hadn't spent the whole summer together, going over to each other's houses almost every day.

"I'd rather think about the semi-formal," said

Pamela. "Summer's still a long way off."

"Who are *you* going with?" Elizabeth asked her. I was going with my boyfriend, Patrick, of course. A guy named Sam, in Camera Club, had asked me too, but Patrick's been my boyfriend since sixth grade, so I guess it was Patrick and me for the dance.

"Aren't you back with Mark?" I asked Pamela. "Aren't you going with him?"

"I'm going to ask somebody new and different," Pamela said. "I'm thinking of asking Donald Sheavers."

"Donald Sheavers?" I gasped. My old boyfriend from Takoma Park, handsome as anything but dumb as a doorknob.

"Going steady is 'out,' Alice. Didn't you know? Everybody goes out with everybody. In a group. And when you *do* go out with a guy alone, you mix it up. I mean, maybe you'll go to a party with him and come home with someone else. You and Patrick have been going together so long you're like an old married couple."

"Hardly," I said.

"It's true! When you only go out with one guy, everyone assumes you're having sex."

"What?" Elizabeth cried.

"Oh, Pamela, that's not true," I said. Sometimes she really ticks me off. Pamela makes these statements like they're true for everyone, and they're not.

"Wait till you get to high school!" she said. "If you're still going with Patrick then, I'll bet kids will talk. Besides, how do you know you won't like other guys better if you never try any of them?"

"I *don't* know. I just hate giving up somebody I really like, that's all," I told her.

"You don't give him up, that's the point, Alice. You share him. And when you choose buffet, you can have something of everything!"

I rolled my eyes.

"How are you going to wear your hair for the dance?" Elizabeth asked me.

"On my head, as usual," I said.

"I'm going to wear mine piled up on top," she said.

"Now *that's* out!" said Pamela. "Everyone says so. We're all going together in the same car, aren't we?"

"Yes! We pile in the car and see how many couples we can squeeze in. That's 'in.' So I've heard, anyway," said Elizabeth.

I wondered if I should start making a list— what's in and what's out. The thing was, I could see already that in some ways I was out. Whenever we read magazines together—Pamela, Elizabeth, and I—I want to turn past the articles on "shaping your brows" and "fabrics that flounce" and go to personality quizzes and stuff. Elizabeth and Pamela are sort of fixated on clothes and hair and makeup, I think. I can take about ten minutes of it, and then I'm bored out of my mind. They've already made phone calls back and forth about what they'll wear to the dance and haven't included me. Then I wonder if they talk about me behind my back—criticize the way I dress and everything. What will happen to us when we get to high school? I wonder. Who will be "in" and who will be "out"?

When I got home, Lester, my twenty-one-year-old brother, was making spaghetti sauce for dinner. I stood in the doorway watching him add the ingredients, and when he started to mash the garlic, I said, "That's 'out,' Lester. Basil's 'in.'"

"Really?" said Les, and put it in anyway.

When Dad came to the table in a blue shirt with white collar and cuffs, I told him those kinds of shirts were out.

"So?" said Dad. "Then I'll have my own special look, won't I?"

It was when I was breaking my breadstick into a dozen different pieces that I realized both Dad and Lester were staring at me.

"Feeding the birds?" asked Dad.

"No. . . ." I took my index finger and idly flicked each piece across my plate, then flicked them in the other direction. "I'm ready for a big change in my life, but not the kind that's happening to me."

"So what's happening to you? Fangs at the full moon, or what?" asked Lester.

"Be serious," I said to both of them. "I just realized that good things don't stay the same. I mean, I can remember when Elizabeth and Pamela and I imagined us all getting summer jobs at the same place and going to the same college and all getting married around the same time and living in the same town. And already we're thinking about doing entirely different things this summer."

"Well, you're not Siamese triplets," Lester said. "You really will continue breathing on your own, you know."

"It's called 'life,' Al, and life is change," Dad said.

"Not all change is good, though," I told him.

"I know," he said.

I started in on my spaghetti, but Lester always puts too many mushrooms in it for me. I like chunky spaghetti sauce with lots of meat in it, and Lester's sort of slides its way down your throat.

"Life should be like a Coke machine," I said.

"You drop in your money and get the same drink over and over again. No surprises."

"You're absolutely profound," said Lester. He's a philosophy major in college, senior year. He switched over from business. "That would be as boring as boiled potatoes."

"Someday it's going to happen to you, Les," I told him. "Marilyn's not going to wait for you forever, you know. You can't just go on ringing her number, thinking she'll always be there. One of these times you'll call up and find out she's married."

"She's not the only woman in the world, Al," Lester said, which was about the same thing Pamela had said about Patrick.

Something good happened after dinner. Aunt Sally called from Chicago and said that she and her daughter—my grown-up cousin Carol, who used to be married to a sailor—were coming to stay with us for five days. Carol would be attending a convention in Washington, D.C., so Aunt Sally was coming along, and she'd cook all our favorite dishes.

"That's great!" I told her. I love having Carol around. She's sophisticated and funny and knows absolutely everything I need to know about life and stuff. The one question I've always wanted to ask her is what it's really, really like to have sex with a man. I couldn't think of a single other person I could ask. I'd be too embarrassed to ask Marilyn Rawley, Lester's girlfriend. Ditto Miss Summers. And I sure wasn't going to ask Aunt Sally, because if she told me once that getting your period was like a moth becoming a butterfly, she'd probably say that sexual intercourse was like a deer getting antlers or something.

Elizabeth's mother told her that sex between a husband and wife is beautiful, but "beautiful" doesn't do anything for me. Pamela read in Ann Landers that Niagara Falls, where a lot of couples go on their honeymoon, is a bride's "second biggest disappointment," meaning, of course, that intercourse is the first. So what *does* it feel like? I've always wondered. As good as a back rub? A kiss? Or is it more like a sneeze or hiccups?

"You're sure you have room, now?" Aunt Sally was asking.

"Of course! Carol can sleep with me!" I told her.

"We'll sleep wherever you put us. It will just be so good to see you all again," said Aunt Sally.

I told Dad and Lester that they were coming, and Les was happy too, because he and Carol get along real well. She's a few years older than he is, and they always kid around. Dad, though, didn't exactly jump for joy, because Aunt Sally is Mom's older sister, and she's probably never quite forgiven him for wooing Mom away from a rich boyfriend named Charlie Snow, and all because Dad wrote such wonderful love letters.

"Is it okay if Carol sleeps with me?" I asked Dad when I told him they were coming.

"If it's all right with Carol," said Dad. "I'm going to put Sal in my bedroom, though, and I'll put up the cot in the dining room for myself."

"Sure you want to do that, Dad? Have her snooping through your things?" Lester asked.

"Everything that's important to me is in that trunk in the attic," Dad said. "I'd rather have Sal confined up in my bedroom than give her the run of the downstairs. She'd be up at the crack of dawn making biscuits."

A week later, I had just finished hosing off the front porch and was mopping it dry when a cab pulled up, and out got Carol and Aunt Sally.

"Hi!" I yelled, throwing down the mop, and ran out to give them both a big hug.

"Alice, you're looking gorgeous!" Carol said, and we both laughed, because I was barefoot, with my jeans rolled up to my knees.

"So are you!" I said, only Carol really was gorgeous. She's on the tall side, with hair about the color of mine—more strawberry, maybe, than blond—and she has *really* green eyes. She was wearing a rayon pant and jacket outfit, and a scarf of a million colors around her neck.

Dad and Lester came out of the house, and when Carol saw Les, she dramatically held out her arms and cried, "Lester!"

He fell right into the act. "Carol!" he said.

She rushed into his arms, and he bent her backward almost all the way to the ground like they do on a dance floor.

Dad sort of chuckled, and Aunt Sally stared, but I laughed. Some people are real live wires, and Carol's one of them.

"Carol, how lovely you look!" said Dad, when she was upright again. "And, Sal, how *are* you?" He hugged them both. "How's Milt?"

"Just as stubborn and wonderful as ever," Aunt Sally said. "He talked about coming, but decided that somebody ought to stay home to feed the cat." Then she hugged us all again. She said she was going to cook supper, Dad said she'd do no such thing, we went inside and ordered takeout, and then sat around the dining room table eating pork lo mein and cashew chicken.

"My, you've certainly fixed up the place since we were here last," said Aunt Sally. "New furniture and all! Ben, you've got excellent taste."

I almost wished she hadn't said anything, because part of the reason Dad bought good furniture was that he'd started dating Sylvia Summers. But for once Aunt Sally showed some tact and didn't bring it up. She focused on Lester instead.

"Lester," she said, scooping out the last cashew from the little white carton, "what is a handsome man like you doing unattached, I'd like to know?"

Aunt Sally has felt for some time that Lester's too flighty when it comes to women and that he should pick one special girl, not just "jump from one to another," as she put it.

"Easy, Sal. He's only twenty-one," Dad said genially.

"And still in school," I put in, "which he will probably be for the rest of his natural life, because after June, he's going to graduate school."

"I didn't say I was in a rush to see him married, but I'd think by now there would be one special lady in his life," said Aunt Sally.

"Same here," I said. "That's what we're all wondering." I grinned at Lester.

I could see the corners of his mouth twitch the way they do when he's about to make a joke, and he looked across the table at Carol and said, "Oh, but there is!"

"Oh, Lester!" said Carol, her voice breaking just a little.

Aunt Sally looked quickly from Lester to Carol,

and I laughed again. The thing about Aunt Sally is she never seems to know when you're joking. Dad told me once that Mom had a great sense of humor. Maybe she got it all and her sister didn't get any, but Aunt Sally's sure fun to tease.

"I heard that one of your old girlfriends got married," Aunt Sally said. "Ben sent me a picture of Alice in her bridesmaid's dress, and I'll confess, I was a little surprised you let Crystal get away."

"She had a greater love for another man. These things happen," Lester said. "More egg rolls, anyone?"

"What about that other girl, the one who works for you, Ben?" asked Aunt Sally.

"Marilyn Rawley," I said helpfully.

"Yes, what about Marilyn?" Aunt Sally just wouldn't shut up. "Are you still seeing her?"

"I was until Carol reentered my life," said Lester.

"Be still, my heart," said Carol, and Dad and I laughed again. This time Aunt Sally laughed a little too.

But it was later, when we'd finished eating and had spread our photo albums on the dining room table, that the joke began to build. Lester was sitting at one end of the table, Carol around the corner from him, and every time they came to a picture of Lester, Carol told him he looked handsome or virile or studly or something. Every time they came to a photo of Carol, Lester said she looked beautiful or voluptuous.

Aunt Sally alternated between falling silent every time they complimented each other or talking too loud and too fast. I went along with the joke by pretending to take it seriously and stopped laughing out loud, even though I was cracking up. It was hard to tell just what Dad was thinking. I guess he was a little puzzled, a little embarrassed, but he figured—hoped, anyway— that it was all in good fun.

After a while Lester and Carol and I migrated to the living room, leaving the photo albums to Dad and Aunt Sal, who knew a lot more of the relatives than we did.

Lester chose an old Katherine Hepburn-Spencer Tracy video to put in the VCR. He and Carol sat on the sofa and I sat cross-legged in the recliner, enjoying their jokes and comments about as much as I did the movie itself.

Lester and Carol are the kind of people who sort of feed each other lines, and if one of them starts a joke, the other can finish it. We were talking about the different kinds of kisses you see on the screen, and every time we came up with a new one, Les and Carol would demonstrate, really exaggerating, making me laugh. They'd gone through the John Wayne kind of kiss to Jimmy

Stewart and Clark Gable to James Bond, and they were demonstrating the Alan Alda kind of kiss when we noticed Dad and Aunt Sally watching wordlessly from the dining room.

"And then there's the lip-brushing style, like this," Carol told me. She put her hands on Lester's shoulders, slowly leaned toward him, and brushed his lips a couple of times with her own before they kissed.

Dad and Aunt Sally got up from the table and came to stand in the doorway, looking disturbed.

Lester and Carol took in the situation immediately.

"Dad, Aunt Sal," Lester said, looking as serious as he could without laughing, "Carol and I have something to tell you."

Carol took over. She reached for Lester's arm, put her cheek against his shoulder for a moment, and said, "Les and I are engaged. We can't keep our love a secret any longer."

Aunt Sally plopped down in a chair, looking dazed. Was it possible, I wondered, that she thought they were serious?

"You're . . . you're *cousins*!" Aunt Sally gasped. "You *can't* marry!"

"Oh, we'll find a state where it's legal, Mom," Carol said.

"Or we could elope," added Lester, his voice

cracking a little, the way it does when he's trying not to laugh.

Dad still didn't say anything. I think he figured that if he just shut up and listened, he'd know whether to worry or not.

"When did you *decide* all this? Carol, you never said a word to me!" Aunt Sally continued.

"Oh, we've been writing back and forth," Carol said, "and Les writes the most beautiful love letters!"

Aunt Sally jerked around and glared at Dad as though it were all his fault.

"Don't look at me, Sal. I'm in the dark here," Dad told her.

Aunt Sally faced Lester and Carol again. "Have you set a date?" she asked.

She *did* believe them! I laughed out loud, and Aunt Sally turned on me next.

"Did *you* know anything about this?" she asked.

"Only that I get to be one of the bridesmaids," I kidded, looking serious again.

"And don't forget to give me your measurements, Alice, so I can order your dress," Carol said, winking at me.

We kept it up for the next five minutes until things got so outrageous that Aunt Sally began to guess, and Dad looked relieved. We never came right out and said we'd been teasing, and I think

Dad wished we hadn't started it in the first place.

I couldn't help but feel a little bit sad for him just then. The trouble with being part of an "in" joke or an "in" crowd is that there has to be somebody who's "out." And you never know how that feels, I guess, until it happens to you.

2

Pillow Talk

Carol went off to her conference the next day. Dad went to work as usual, I went to school, and Lester went to his classes at the university. When Les and I got home that afternoon, Aunt Sal had baked a pie and a few dozen peanut butter cookies. A note on the table said she was off to the store for yeast.

"Do you get yeast infections from yeast?" I asked Lester.

"Don't look at me," said Lester. "That's a female thing. We jocks just itch."

We each had a couple of cookies and chugged down a bottle of Sprite. Then I said, "When you were kidding around with Carol last night, did you feel anything?"

Lester wiped his mouth on his sleeve and raised an eyebrow at me. "What do you mean, did I *feel* anything? Did I fondle her, do you mean?"

"No, I mean, did you feel lust?"

"*Lust?* Who are you, Queen Victoria?"

"Sexy. Did it *excite* you, Lester? Do I have to spell it out?"

"If you mean did it turn me on, sure, a little. Do you mean did I want to throw her on her back and make mad love? No."

"But isn't that what grown-ups worry about—that sex ed classes will excite us so much, we'll all bolt from the classroom and head for the bushes or something?"

"I've got news," said Lester. "There's nothing that takes the excitement out of sex faster than a sex ed class. Listen, kiddo, if I did everything my impulses told me to do, I'd go make love to the cashier down at the 7-Eleven, tell off my philosophy prof, shoot the guy who almost sideswiped me on the beltway this morning, and I would have gotten rid of *you* years ago. Held your head under water or something."

"Thanks, Les, I love you too," I said.

When Aunt Sally got back from the store, she said that yeast was for baking bread. After that she was going to make brownies, then applesauce and a pork roast.

"And after that," joked Lester, "the world!"

It was different having Aunt Sally and Carol around, even though they only stayed for five days. I wasn't the only female in the house, for one thing. After dinner, when Dad and Aunt Sally stayed at the table talking, Carol and Les and I would do the dishes or watch TV or kid around in the living room. I figured this is how it would feel to have a dad *and* a mom, an older brother *and* a sister. It wouldn't just be Dad and Les studying *me* at the table each night, waiting for me to say something stupid. We could concentrate on Carol for a change.

I was sure concentrating on Carol. I'd pushed my clothes from one side of my closet so Carol could hang hers in there, and emptied two drawers of my dresser. Carol got up really early each morning, even before I did, and after she took a shower, she'd come back to the bedroom, slip off her robe, and put on her panties and bra.

The first morning I had my eyes half-closed, but when a twenty-five-year-old woman is standing stark naked in front of you, I think you're allowed a peek.

You can learn a lot just by looking, you know. For one thing, I learned how to put on a bra. When *I* put on a bra, I just hook it behind me. But when a grown woman with huge breasts puts on a bra, she slips the straps over her shoulders, then leans over and lets her breasts *fall* into the bra cups before she hooks it. *So* that's *the way you get your nipples where they're supposed to be,* I thought. Half the time I put on a bra and my nipples are over or under where I want them. I couldn't wait to tell Elizabeth and Pamela all I was learning.

Carol, of course, didn't know I was watching her, and I don't think she would have cared if she knew. She'd put a couple of squirts of cologne between her breasts, and talcum powder beneath them. I figured maybe she had learned how to drop her breasts into a bra and powder beneath them by watching other women do it, just the way I was watching her.

At night she'd pull on a silk nightshirt that came halfway down her thighs, or maybe a long T-shirt, and then she'd crawl under the blanket and we'd tell each other stuff, and I decided that before she and her mother went back to Chicago, I would ask the question I'd been wanting to know ever since I was nine years old, practically: What is sexual intercourse really, really like for a woman? That's why I couldn't ask Dad or Lester.

Still, how do you just come right out and ask a question like that? Lester says I'm a social ignoramus—I just blurt stuff out. So I tried to think of a way I could ask it tactfully.

The first night that Carol and I shared my bed, we talked about all the crazy things we could remember that Lester had done when he was growing up. Carol told me about the time he stuck a vitamin pill up one nostril and couldn't get it out, and all day he dripped purple snot. The second night we talked about trips we'd taken, places we'd been. Our best vacations. Stuff like that. Carol, of course, has been lots and lots of places, and I've hardly been anywhere, so she did most of the talking.

The third night I tried to get the conversation on weddings. I figured if we could talk about that, I could steer it around to honeymoons, and if I could get Carol talking about honeymoons, then we could talk about sex. I mean, I read somewhere that the average woman has sexual intercourse 3,948 times in her life, and I have a right to know what I'll be getting myself into. But we didn't talk about any of it. Carol talked about her job instead, and I fell asleep in the middle.

The last night, I knew it was the only chance I'd get to ask my question. So when Carol said something about her ex-husband, the sailor—about the kind of music he liked—I said, "Carol, maybe it's none of my business, but why did you get a divorce?"

"Because he was a jerk," she said.

"Then why did you marry him?"

"Because I didn't know it then. I thought that as

soon as he quit the navy, he'd settle down. Well, he didn't. He went right on being a sailor."

"What do you mean? He kept going out to sea?"

"He was out to sea, all right. He was out to lunch! He'd go off for a couple of days at a time with his buddies, like I'd always be waiting for him when he got back. Well, one day he came home and I wasn't. We got married too young, Alice. I married him because he was cute. And 'cute' is about the least important thing in a marriage, take my word for it."

"What *is* important, then?"

"Hmm." Carol adjusted the pillow behind her head. "I guess what's important is that you feel pretty much the same about the really big things—children and religion and politics and money—and that you respect each other's differences about the rest."

"Is sex a really big thing?"

"Sure. Though some people feel it's more important than others do."

"How do you know how important it's going to be?"

"I guess you just talk with each other about it— get to know each other really well before you marry. If that's all a guy seems to think about, and you don't share a lot of other stuff together, then that tells you a lot about him right there."

I swallowed. "Carol, what does intercourse really, really feel like for a woman?"

There. The question was out. The room was awfully quiet.

"The first time, you mean?" she asked.

"Well, yes. That too."

"Uh . . . Alice, you *do* know how it's done, don't you? I mean . . ."

"I know what goes where," I told her. "But how does it *feel* when a man's penis goes inside you?"

"Well, for some women it hurts a little the first time. Maybe the first couple of times. After that it doesn't. It feels pretty good, actually. It's exciting to feel yourself opening up for a man, and nice to have him kissing you."

"But you spend your whole honeymoon in pain? Is that why people go away somewhere and lie on the beach?"

She laughed. "Not exactly. Besides, so many girls use tampons now that they've already stretched themselves a little down there. A honeymoon's sort of a vacation after all the work of a wedding. It used to be that a man and woman felt self-conscious and shy right after they were married, so they went off to be alone where people weren't always watching them."

"Okay, but what's sex like later? When it doesn't

hurt anymore?" It was easy to ask questions in the dark, I discovered.

"Such questions!" Carol said.

"You're the only one I can ask," I told her. "I've always wanted to know. Pamela and Elizabeth do too. All we know is what we see in the movies, and the movies make it look as though a man and a woman are having a fit together."

Carol laughed again, then rolled over and faced me in the darkened room. "Forget movies, Alice. They aren't much help. It looks so easy in the movies. A man and woman climb in bed and make wild love and they both come at the same time and—"

"What does that mean?"

"An orgasm. A climax. A peak of excitement. If you've ever masturbated, you already know what it feels like."

"So how is real life different from the movies?" I asked.

"Whew! These questions really *are* getting embarrassing," she said.

"Okay. I'm sorry. I'll just go on being a sexual ignoramus the rest of my life, and on my wedding night I'll tell my husband I'm a lot stupider than he thought, because I couldn't find anyone who would—"

"Okay, okay," Carol said. "In the movies, a couple

has intercourse, and the man and woman climax at the same time. In real life, some men and women like to make love in other ways. Every woman is different, so it's up to her to tell her partner what she really likes. Same goes for the man. That's one of the problems with having sex with someone you don't know too well."

"Why?"

"Because girls want guys to think they're sexy, so they sigh and moan and do all the stuff they see women do in the movies. Then the guy thinks he's a real stud, so he goes right on doing what feels good to him, and it may never do much for the girl. Wait for someone you really love, Alice— love enough to marry—and then you can talk about things like that."

I swallowed. It was embarrassing enough trying to imagine Patrick and me, for example, having sexual intercourse. I couldn't even imagine having to give him instructions!

"I don't think I can do that, Carol," I said finally. "It's too embarrassing."

"Alice! You're thirteen! Of course it's embarrassing!"

"Fourteen," I corrected. "Almost."

"You don't have to think about these things for years yet! It would have been embarrassing for me at fourteen too. Heck, it was embarrassing enough at nineteen when I married The Jerk. The main thing about sex is that you should feel comfortable and just enjoy being together, touching and kissing and not worrying too much about the rest. If a man really loves you, he'll want to keep you happy and will make love how ever you want."

I thought about that awhile. "If I *don't* like intercourse so much, what are the *other* ways?"

"Almost anything you can imagine. Sometimes you may want your husband to touch you with his hands and sometimes with his lips, and you'll try different things and see what's best. You'll want to ask him what he'd like *you* to do to *him*. You're just two people in love, giving each other pleasure."

We lay so long then without talking that I realized finally Carol had fallen asleep. Her breathing came slower, more steady, and one of her legs gave a little twitch. Sex was a lot more complicated than I had thought. I'd always imagined that the woman just lay down on her back, and the man got on top of her, and something wonderful happened. All the woman had to do was wear a sexy nightgown. I never imagined she had to talk! To give directions, yet!

Elizabeth invited Pamela and me for a sleepover Sunday after Aunt Sally and Carol flew back to Chicago. We were sitting there cross-legged on Elizabeth's bed—one of the two twin beds with white ruffles in her room—and were eating Pringles when I said, "Well, I asked the question."

"What question?" asked Pamela, her mouth full of chips.

"About sex. What intercourse is really, really like."

Elizabeth looked embarrassed already. "Do we have to discuss this?" she asked.

"No, Elizabeth. Pamela and I can sit in the bathroom and talk about it, and you can go your whole life not knowing what to expect on your wedding night," I said.

"All right, go on then," she said reluctantly.

"I already know what sex is like," said Pamela. "I see it on the adult channel all the time. Men groan and women moan and then they both smoke cigarettes."

"Wrong," I said, and for once I knew something Pamela didn't. "That's the movie version, Pamela. That's not real life."

Pamela leaned back against one of the pillows. "Well, I know that once you start having sex, you're addicted," she said. "When mothers write to Ann Landers to say their teenage daughters are having sex, Ann says you'd better make sure they know all about birth control, because once they start, they can't stop."

"What?" cried Elizabeth, alarmed. "Like perpetual motion or something?"

"Oh, Pamela!" I scolded. Pamela always exaggerates.

"Okay, what is sex really, really like? Carol should know," she said.

"Well," I told her importantly, "it's the same kind of climax you feel if you touch yourself, except you have a man kissing you too, which makes it more exciting. Some people like intercourse best, and some people like other things, and it doesn't matter what."

"You mean you can try a whole bunch of stuff to see what you like the most?" asked Pamela, looking interested.

"I don't even want to think about it," said Elizabeth.

"The main thing, Carol said, is that a woman sort of has to give a man directions—tell him where to touch her and everything," I said.

Elizabeth looked horrified. In fact, she choked on a Pringle. "You have to *talk* about it? Out loud?"

"You could probably type it on a piece of paper," Pamela told her.

"I can't do this!" Elizabeth gasped. "I won't!"

"Carol would say that if you can't talk about things like this with a man, then you shouldn't be in bed with him in the first place. She says if a man really loves you, he'll make love any way you want." And then I added jokingly, "Standing on his head, even!"

We were all quiet. Elizabeth had her eyes tightly closed. I think we'd *all* had the idea that with sex, women just let it happen.

"Whoever invented sex must have had a sense of humor," I said at last.

And Pamela said, "Why couldn't we make love like amoebas—just dissolve together and not have to worry about giving instructions?"

"Why couldn't we make babies just by shaking hands?" said Elizabeth. "Why do our sexual parts have to be down *there,* for heaven's sake?"

"And if sex isn't like it is in the movies, why do women keep on getting married and having intercourse? They must like something about it," Pamela said.

"Maybe they like having somebody to snuggle up to on cold nights," I suggested. "Maybe it's nice having somebody around to talk to and do things with—plan a life together and everything."

"Maybe what they really want is children," said Elizabeth.

Pamela began to grin. "And maybe they really do

like to take off their clothes and get naked together and have sex and make love no matter *how* they do it. By land or sea, underwater, in the air, in the trees. . . ."

"Whatever works," I said.

The more we thought about it, the better it seemed. If I got married when I was twenty-five, say, that gave me at least eleven years to get used to telling my future husband how I wanted him to make love to me. Once I figured it out myself, I mean.

We turned on Elizabeth's TV and saw a man and woman starting to make love. The woman's hair wasn't even messed up. She had gorgeous breasts. Their bedroom overlooked the sea. Gulls were calling. The man was groaning, the woman was moaning, and waves crashed up on the shore.

"Get serious," I said to the couple on TV.

"Get real," said Pamela.

"Get another channel," said Elizabeth.

So we did.

3

A Startling Announcement

I worried that Dad might find the house sort of quiet and depressing after Carol and Aunt Sally went home. He's always saying we need more stimulating conversation at mealtimes, so when I came to the table Monday evening, I said, "March twenty-first is the International Day for the Elimination of Racial Prejudice."

"Oh?" said Dad. "I didn't realize that."

"Never heard of it," said Lester. "Are we supposed to put up a flag or something?"

"For your information," I told him, "we learned about it from Mrs. Willis in social studies. The U.N. started it in 1966 to remember everyone who has ever been the victim of racial prejudice."

"Very noble indeed," said Dad, and passed the applesauce.

Actually, Patrick told me that they'd discussed it in Student Council, and the real reason we were

observing March 21 was that a couple of neigh-
borhoods in Montgomery County had experi-
enced racial incidents. Our school decided to
head them off before they started, and get kids
thinking about prejudice now.

Our school is about two-thirds white. The rest
are mostly African American or Asian. I hadn't
paid much attention to this before because I usually hung out with kids I'd known from elemen-
tary school. Everyone had sort of his own special
group. There were the really smart kids, the
Brains; the sports kids, the Jocks; the Bikers—a
bunch of guys who bleached their hair and rode
dirt bikes to school; the Barbs—a group of flashily
dressed girls with money . . . I guess that up until
now, each group didn't pay much attention to
anyone else.

"Anyway, the school's making a big deal of it
this semester," I went on. "We've been talking
about prejudice a lot, and how you deal with it."

"I didn't know that was a particular problem in
your school," said Dad.

"It isn't! There's a lot more prejudice toward
kids who don't have the right clothes than there is
toward minorities. Last September the guys were
teasing some poor seventh-grader who came to
school with a Darth Vader backpack. They asked if
it belonged to his kid brother."

"Ye gods," said Lester. "Now it's not enough to have the right jacket or the right shoes? You have to have the right backpack? What is this? The army?"

"There's one small difference in that kind of discrimination," said Dad. "If you don't have the kind of clothes that happen to be 'in,' there's always the possibility of getting them. But if your skin color isn't 'in,' you're stuck."

"Well, I certainly haven't seen that kind of prejudice in our school," I said.

"You being a green-eyed strawberry blonde, I doubt you would," Dad told me.

What I don't like is the way Dad and Lester talk about *my* generation, and *my* school, when they don't know anything about it. Lester isn't my age! Dad doesn't go to my school! What do they know?

"There isn't any prejudice at my school!" I declared hotly. "Everybody gets along."

"I'm glad to hear it," said Dad.

"One big happy family, huh?" said Lester. "As long as you have the right backpack?"

"We're doing just fine," I retorted.

I noticed, though, that I went out of my way on Tuesday to talk with Gwen, the short black girl in my math class. She's the brain in general math, and she helps me sometimes when I'm stuck on something.

"How's it going?" I asked, falling in beside her on the way to gym. She's the one who told me about being a candy striper too.

"Heavy," she said, flashing a smile. "I've got one too many courses. I think I'd do fine if I just had one less thing to study at night."

"Wait'll we get to high school," I moaned.

"Yeah, that's what's worrying me," she said.

"You taking college prep, then?"

"Sure."

"Do you know what you want to do?"

"Uh-uh. Not really. I'm *thinking* about teaching. I always wanted to be a singer, but you have to be really, really good to make it big time. I'll probably settle for second best and be a music teacher." She glanced at me. "Do you sing?"

"Are you kidding? I'm the only member of my family who can't carry a tune."

She laughed. "You go with that drummer, don't you?"

"Yeah, Patrick. He can't understand me, either."

We went to our lockers, still smiling. *See?* I told myself. *Where's the prejudice here?*

It was when I got to social studies that afternoon that I heard about what we were going to do the week of March 21. Mrs. Willis talked about the many target groups of prejudice based on race or sex or age or money, and that the week of March 21 would be declared Consciousness-Raising Week, or CRW, for the whole school.

In fifth-period class that day, every student was handed a list of rules for CRW, during which the school would be run by an arbitrary sort of caste system based on the color of the student's hair.

Mr. Ormand, our principal, came over the public-address system and explained it to us. This was only an experiment in consciousness-raising, he said. Every student, in every class, had to turn in a one-page essay at the end of the week on how he or she felt during CRW. And then he read the rules aloud while we followed along on our instruction sheets.

Those with dark brown or black hair were the A group.

Those with light brown hair, red hair, or dark blond were group B.

Those with light blond or gray hair were the C group.

The A's, Mr. Ormand said, were to be the privileged group. Only the A's could use the front staircase. The B's had to use the stairs at the side or back, and the C's could use only the back staircase.

The A's got to sit at the tables in the center of the cafeteria next to the salad bar and the ice-cream table. The B's had to use the tables on either side, and the C's were confined to the tables at one end. The A's got to board the buses first, then the B's, then the C's.

And so it went. Everyone laughed, because it seemed so ridiculous. But to make sure everyone knew exactly what caste he or she belonged to, the fifth-period teachers passed out colored paper circles, which we had to pin to our clothes every day.

Elizabeth, with her long dark hair and eyelashes, got a big gold circle with an A in the center. I got an orange circle with a B in it. Pamela, with her short blond feather cut, got a white circle with a large black C in the center.

"What caste are you?" Patrick asked me when we went to the bus after school. "I'm a B."

"So am I," I told him. "What a joke! Teachers think up some pretty weird stuff sometimes."

"I think that's what they do on those in-service training days, sit around and figure out how they can make our lives miserable," said Brian, who *used* to be the handsomest guy in school until Justin Collier came along, the boy who's taking Elizabeth to the dance.

"You don't see *them* wearing circles," said Elizabeth, who didn't have a thing to worry about because she was an A.

"Yes, you do," Pamela told me. "I heard Miss Summers say she was a B. She and Mr. Everett were wondering what Mr. Ormand would be, because he's bald as a cue ball."

"He's probably the one who thought the whole thing up. He can just sit back and play God," said Brian.

Patrick slid onto the seat beside me. He's got red hair—more like orange bronze. The hair on his arms and legs is orange too. He told me once that his mom was a ravishing redhead when she was younger.

"So was mine," I said. "A redhead, anyway. More like me—strawberry blond. She was taller, though."

"Do you remember her much?" asked Patrick.

"No. I wish I did. She liked to sing, and she wore slacks a lot. That's what they tell me. I get my memories of her all mixed up with Aunt Sally, who took care of us for a while after Mom died. I was in kindergarten. I guess you don't remember too much before then."

Elizabeth leaned over the back of our seat. "This isn't a very good idea," she said. "Everyone will be walking around wearing circles, like in a Jewish ghetto or something."

"Or the caste system in India," said Patrick, who has lived in a lot of different countries because his dad works for the State Department. "I think it will be interesting."

"*I* think it will be embarrassing," said Elizabeth. "I don't know why I should get all these special privileges just because I'm a brunette."

"That's the whole point," said Patrick. "You shouldn't. It doesn't make any sense."

Pamela turned around and got up on her knees on the seat in front of us. "Then if it doesn't make sense, why do it? I can see trying it for a day, maybe, but a week. . . ."

"So put that down in your essay," Patrick told her. "Maybe you'll end up with an *A* and all the *A*'s will get *C*'s on their reports. That would be justice." He laughed.

"Oh, it'll be a blast," Pamela decided. "I can be late for every single class because I have to use the back staircase, and no one can say a thing. If I have to be discriminated against, then I'm going to have some fun."

It *would* be sort of fun, I thought. Something different.

When I told Dad and Lester later exactly how CRW was going to work, Dad said he had great admiration for our school. "They ought to try that in every school in Montgomery County!" he said. "It ought to be a required project in every school in Maryland. In the country!"

But Lester raised one eyebrow at me. "So what are you? One of the privileged class?"

"For your information, I'm a B," I told him. "That's one level down. So's Patrick. Only the people with dark hair get to be number one, the A's."

Dad wanted to know all the details, of course— whether the teachers had to participate and whether Miss Summers was a B. But Lester seemed distracted. He sat hunched over his Hamburger Helper, and finally, when I had managed to bore them both silly, he said, "I thought the two of you might like to know that Marilyn and I are no longer 'an item,' as they say."

We just looked at him, waiting.

"Oh? That's news," Dad said finally. "Was this by mutual agreement, Les, or should I ask?"

"We agreed, more or less. I suggested it, actually. I guess I felt that she'd been getting too serious about us, and I didn't want any hurt feelings."

I'm only thirteen-going-on-fourteen, but I know this much: If Lester thought that by cutting Marilyn off at the pass he could avoid hurt feelings, then he still believed in the tooth fairy.

"I've got news for you, Les," I said. "She's hurt already."

"Why? You've talked to Marilyn?"

"I *know* Marilyn. She's been going with you for two and a half years, and I'll bet anything she hoped it would amount to something."

"I never led her on," said Lester. "I never said anything that would encourage her to think we'd be getting engaged."

"Yes, but by spending so much time with her, isn't there a possibility she thought you were more serious than you are?" asked Dad.

"Then that's her problem, Dad. How do you know if a woman is right for you unless you do spend a lot of time together?"

"But . . . two and a half years?" asked Dad.

"I was seeing other women too, you know. Crystal . . ."

"And Joy. Don't forget Joy," I said, remembering a dingbat Lester brought to a birthday party I gave once for Dad.

"But did Marilyn know about them?" Dad asked him.

"Some of them, yes. Listen, Dad, what do you want me to do?" Lester asked. "Marry Marilyn just so I won't hurt her feelings?"

"Of course not. You're doing the right thing, Les. But I also believe that Alice is right when she says that Marilyn's probably taking it harder than you think."

❋ ❋ ❋ ❋

Lester didn't know the half of it.

I work for three hours on Saturday mornings at my dad's music store, the Melody Inn, and this time when I got there, Marilyn, who's in charge of the Gift Shoppe, was back behind the counter, a tissue tucked tightly in her hand, her eyes as red as strawberries.

"I heard," I told her.

Her eyes flashed, and I sure hoped she wasn't going to be mad at *me*. She's one of the best employees Dad ever hired because she knows about all kinds of music—folk and rock and classical and stuff—and Dad's always been afraid of what might happen if she and Lester broke up.

"Did he tell you I've invested two and a half years of my life in that guy, and he's dropped me like a dirty sock?" she asked.

For Lester's sake, I tried to set the record straight. "Well, it wasn't exactly two and a half years," I told her. "I mean, he was going out with Crystal Harkins and a dingbat from school part of that time too."

"That's supposed to make me feel better?" Marilyn snapped. "It wouldn't surprise me one bit if Crystal was behind all this."

I stared at Marilyn as I began cleaning the glass of the gift wheel. "What do you mean?"

"I've heard rumors she's not happy. I'll bet she's making a play for Lester again."

Was it possible? I wondered. I remembered how Crystal had called Lester recently. . . .

Marilyn turned away and covered her face with her hands. I was glad we didn't have any customers yet, because she looked so sad, it almost made *me* cry.

"I . . . I loved him, Alice! He was so gentle and sweet and funny when we were together," she wept. "If he goes back to Crystal, he'll not only break my heart, he'll break up her marriage for sure."

"The dog!" I said indignantly.

"And then he'll probably drop *her* and break her heart all over again."

"The swine!" I cried.

"I don't know why women are so competitive, Alice. We're all buddy-buddy until it comes to men, and then it's every woman for herself. Crystal already has Peter. Why does she have to take my boyfriend too? Whatever happened to the Sisterhood, all of us looking out for each other, that's what I'd like to know."

By the time I finished work at the Melody Inn and got home, Lester was just coming down to breakfast. Every other Saturday he works at

Maytag selling washing machines, and this was his Saturday off. He was wearing his Mickey Mouse shorts and a T-shirt, and his eyes were only half-open. I didn't care if he *was* only half-awake! I stood in the doorway with my arms folded across my chest and watched him stumble over a chair trying to find the refrigerator.

"Lester," I said, glaring, "I have to know: Are you a home-wrecker or not?"

Lester came to a stop in the middle of the kitchen, his head weaving around, trying to figure out where the voice was coming from.

"You looking for a demolition company, or would you be addressing me?" he asked. He took out a carton of milk and retrieved a box of Cheerios from the cupboard.

"I'm addressing you, Lester, and I think you ought to stop right now before you break any more hearts."

Lester slid sideways onto the chair and filled his bowl to overflowing. "You going to tell me what the heck you're talking about, or do I have to guess?"

"You know very well what I'm talking about! The minister said 'whom God has joined together, let no man put asunder,' and if you're planning to plunder the castle and run off with the bride . . ." I felt like crying.

"What the heck did you have for breakfast, Al? LSD? *What* castle? *What* bride?"

"You're not going back to Crystal?"

"Al, I can't even commit to an unattached female. Why would I get involved with a married woman?" He took a bite and continued staring at me. "You've been talking to Marilyn, right?"

"You told her you *loved* her, Les!" I said accusingly.

"I did!"

"And I'll bet you told Crystal the same thing before she married."

"I did! I loved her too!"

"See?" I said. "I'll bet there were even more girls you said you loved."

"A couple, maybe," Lester told me. "Can I help it if I love women? Can you help it if you love chocolate?"

"Well, the Sisterhood doesn't like your behavior, and we just want you to know that we will be watching your every move. We're going to look out for each other, Lester, and whatever you do or say will be passed along from one female to another. I just want you to know that."

"For the love of Mike!" said Lester, throwing down his spoon. He got up and left the kitchen, but a moment later stuck his head back through the doorway. "I have to go wee-wee, Alice," he said. "Pass it along."

4

We went to school on Monday with our gold or orange or white circles pinned on our shirts, and in a holiday frame of mind. Anything to add a little variety to the week. I think that's one reason they have us change classrooms in January. We go on taking the same courses we started with in September, but with different classmates and teachers. Just so we won't get too bored—so we won't form cliques and stuff.

"Hey, Patrick, where's your circle?" Mark Stedmeister called when we got on the bus.

"Forgot it," Patrick said.

"Well, don't think you can squeeze into group A, 'cause your hair's way too light," Mark told him.

"Yeah? Look at Pamela's. Now *that's* light," Patrick argued.

"*Re*-ject!" someone said to Pamela, and we all laughed.

"What do I care?" said Pamela. "Maybe I'll hang out with the Bikers or something."

"Pamela, you wouldn't!" Elizabeth said.

Everyone who forgot to pin on a circle got another as soon as they walked in the door. Teachers were all over the place handing them out, and they were wearing them too. Patrick tried to argue that he was a dark redhead, but it didn't stick. He got group B's orange circle, just the way I did.

Sam, from Camera Club, had called me over the weekend and said he was supposed to remind members to bring their cameras to school all week. The school newspaper wanted to run a double-page spread of photos—faces and scenes from CRW. They'd take the ten best photos we turned in, so I had my camera and 400 film in my backpack.

At first it wasn't the rules so much that irritated me, it was just trying to remember them all. Where to sit, what staircase to use, what table. Only the A's could use the newer refrigerated drinking fountains, for example. The rest of us had to use the old ceramic fountains that had been there since Year One. The bowls were stained, and the water was warm. Signs over the drinking fountains reminded us: GROUP A ONLY or GOLDS ONLY. Anyone who was African American or Asian had it made. The really light blondes were out of luck.

I started to sit at Elizabeth's table at lunch only to be jeered at by the other dark-haired girls sitting there, and I had to go to a table off to one side. Pamela had to sit way, way back, beside a girl named Leslie, who's probably the blondest blonde in the whole school.

Elizabeth got up and came over. "I feel *horrible* about getting all the good stuff," she said. "It's so stupid."

"Don't worry about it, Elizabeth. Nobody's going to hold it against you," I said.

"So how was the first day of the big experiment?" Dad asked that evening.

"Pretty dumb," I told him. "By the end of the day everyone was using whatever staircase and drinking fountain they wanted, and nobody cared. I *told* you we aren't prejudiced at my school."

The next day, though, there were hall monitors enforcing the rules. They were stationed at every drinking fountain, every staircase, and now the rest rooms had been segregated too. GROUP A ONLY signs were all over the place. The only rest room the kids with white circles could use was in the basement. If you were a B and tried to go up an A staircase, a hall monitor would stop you and say, "Sorry. Golds only." If you were a C and tried to sneak in an A or B rest room, a hall monitor would say, "Use the one in the basement."

It wasn't quite so easy anymore to pretend it was fun, because it *wasn't* fun to run clear down to the other end of the building before the bell. It wasn't fun, after a sweaty game of volleyball in gym, to have to drink warm water from a dingy fountain.

But it was when the cafeteria women said they had run out of bacon cheeseburgers after the Golds had been served that really got to us. The rest of us had to take turkey roll or tuna. Tempers flared just a little, and I got a camera shot of the B's and C's waiting in line, staring enviously at the A's who were enjoying fat, juicy burgers of which we got only the aroma.

"You never ran out of bacon burgers before," one of the bleached-blond Bikers said when he got up to the serving table.

"It happens," was all the cook said.

"Yeah. On purpose," the boy said, shoving the tuna sandwich back at her and stalking out of the cafeteria.

By Wednesday, we were ready for the experiment to be over.

"Okay, they made their point," Pamela said on the bus going home. "Prejudice stinks and discrimination is unfair and we should all love one another, so enough already! If I can't hang out with anyone but blondes, they'll be sorry."

On Thursday, though, teachers took over as hall monitors, and Mr. Ormand himself guarded the front stairs. Mr. Sorringer, our assistant principal—the guy who loves Miss Summers too, but not as much as my dad does, I'll bet—was taking names of anyone who came to school without their colored circle.

I heard that a fight broke out second period, only I didn't see it. The rumor was that a couple of C's jumped a couple of A's who jeered them when they were turned back at the front staircase, but Ormand broke it up in a hurry. I don't know if it really happened, but what I did notice was that things were a lot more tense than they'd been on Monday. Worse, the A's, the ones with the gold circles, had started acting so cliquish. Even Elizabeth. She'd been palling around with Gwen, and when I went to their table once to ask Gwen about an assignment—I didn't even try to sit down—Gwen gave a short answer, then turned back to her conversation with Elizabeth. Maybe I was overreacting, but I felt shut out.

A tall brunette in my English class was nice to me, though. I'd noticed her studying me before, and I guess she felt genuinely sorry for the Oranges and Whites. She walked beside me after English Thursday afternoon and said, "I'm Lori

Haynes. I'll be glad when this week's over, won't you?"

"Will you?" I said. "You've been getting all the perks."

"Yeah, but I know how it feels to be on the other end," she said, though I couldn't imagine why. She wasn't beautiful, but she certainly wasn't ugly. Maybe it was because she was tall, I decided. Never having been tall, I guess you could feel sort of discriminated against, especially if boys avoided you.

"The idea of CRW is okay," I told her, "but I think it's going on a little too long. A couple of days would have been enough. We get the idea."

"Yeah, probably," Lori said. "Though I like it better than our poetry unit in English."

"I'm not big on poems, either," I said. "I disgraced myself last year in Miss Summers's class. We were supposed to recite a favorite poem aloud, and not only did I get mixed up and start reciting the wrong one, but I started crying right in the middle. Can you imagine? I think that's probably one of the most embarrassing things that ever happened to me."

She laughed. "How about wetting your pants in public? *That's* the most embarrassing thing that ever happened to me. I laughed too hard, and then I had to wait until everyone else went home because I didn't dare stand up."

I grinned. "One more day," I said, as we went to our lockers in gym.

"Yeah," she said. "See you."

There were still some nice people left in school, I thought, feeling a little disgruntled at both Gwen and Elizabeth. It was as though people began to accept the idea that they were privileged, a cut above the rest. And Pamela, true to her threat, deserted Leslie and the other blondes and began to hang around with the Bikers, who always ate their lunch outside on the steps, even in winter. She wore a short T-shirt that exposed her midriff and laughed as the guys rode their mountain bikes around the school parking lot, doing wheelies, each trying to upstage the others. Pamela cheered them on and acted as though they were the most interesting people she'd ever met.

"That's disgusting!" I heard Elizabeth say that noon, as I passed her in the hall. Elizabeth was looking out the window at Pamela, who was on the steps below, her arm draped over some guy's shoulder. "I wouldn't be surprised if she got a tattoo! She's being ridiculous!"

"Not any more than you are," I retorted.

She jerked around and stared with wide eyes. "What are you talking about?"

"Just the way you hang around with the other

Golds. You and Gwen purposely shut me out."

"You're imagining things," Elizabeth snapped, and, turning her back to me, walked off to the library.

In the space of only a few days, Elizabeth, Pamela, and I seemed to have drifted apart. Pamela was hanging out with the Bikers, trying to act sexy; Elizabeth was hanging out with Gwen and the other brunettes, acting superior; and I don't know when I'd ever felt so shut out.

"Trouble?" Lori said, falling in beside me as I moved off in the opposite direction.

"Yeah, one of my best friends thinks she's too good for me. She doesn't even realize she's changed."

"That can really hurt," said Lori. "Anyway, I like your sweater. You look good in green. Anybody ever tell you that?"

I smiled then. "Miss Summers did once. She called me Alice Green Eyes. I guess green is my favorite color. What's yours?"

"I don't know. I wear a lot of black because I inherit my brothers' shirts, and they're into black right now. Sometimes I feel like an executioner."

We laughed, and I was grateful that *some*body could put some humor into the day.

The other thing that made CRW bearable, though, was that I caught some really good expressions with my camera—at least I hoped I did. It was a way to forget that I was one of the untouchables, and let my camera do the talking for me. The faces of the Whites standing in line at the one ceramic drinking fountain outside the gym; faces of the girls at the Golds' table, laughing and enjoying their lunch; the face of a guy being turned away from the B staircase. . . .

Sam was everywhere with his camera. With his dark hair, he was one of the Golds, but he hardly seemed to notice. I guess when you're really dedicated to something, the way Sam is to photography, you become very focused. I knew that he'd probably have the best pictures of any of us.

We had barely got to homeroom on Friday when there was an announcement that first-period classes were being suspended for the morning and that we were to spend first period in homeroom instead. I had Mrs. Willis for homeroom, and as soon as Mr. Ormand stopped talking over the school speaker, she stood up and came around to sit on the edge of her desk.

Mrs. Willis is Mexican, I think, married to an Irishman or Scotsman or something, and I saw that she had already removed the gold circle from her dress. She invited us all to remove the circles from our clothes too. I sure was happy to get rid of mine.

"So how was your week?" she asked.

That was met with groans and laughter.

"I'm glad it's over," Leslie said.

"Well, it's not quite over," she told us. "But how did you feel? What did you discover about yourselves? Your friends?"

"I thought it was a joke at first," said a guy, "but I was really pissed . . . uh . . . I mean, ticked off . . . when some of the guys in the gold group tried to keep it going at the mall. Told me I couldn't use the escalator—that kind of stuff. I actually took a swing at somebody. Then we saw security moving in and stopped."

"Things could have gotten out of hand so easily," said Lori.

Mrs. Willis nodded. "That's true. They could. It's the first time we've tried it at this school, and we were a little uneasy ourselves. There were times when I felt the other teachers really resented me, because I could go anywhere I wanted and be served first in the cafeteria. And then I wondered if I was only imagining it."

"You weren't imagining it," I told her. "I resented all the Golds. They got so thick with each other, as though they really deserved special treatment. I guess we were supposed to learn that this is the way prejudice begins."

"I imagine it begins in a dozen different ways.

One of the ways is to be *told* you're superior, or inferior, and you almost start to believe it," said the teacher.

"What got me was that the whole thing was based on something so ridiculous—a little colored circle—and yet the Golds fell right into it. I mean, there was a certain amount of satisfaction. You can't tell me they didn't enjoy it," a boy said.

But a girl from group A countered, "Heck, why not? *We* didn't make the rules."

"Yeah, but you didn't have to go along with them," Leslie told her.

"We did so, or *we'd* get in trouble."

"Bullshit!" someone yelled. Tempers were really flaring now.

"Not one rule said anything about something happening to you if you fraternized with an Orange or a White. The Golds saw a chance to feel superior, and they took it," I agreed.

Mrs. Willis let us go on like this for about twenty minutes, and then, five minutes before the bell, she picked up a box on her desk and started down the aisle, passing out circles again. We couldn't believe it! We all began to protest.

"For the remainder of the day, everyone who was a Gold before is now a White. Everyone who was a White or an Orange before is now a Gold," she said.

"All *right!*" someone yelped, as cheers went up from the former Whites and Oranges. All the Golds looked sheepish.

I met Sam in the hall.

"I got a shot of the faces just after she announced the switch," he said. "Man, I hope it turns out."

"I was too surprised to think of my camera," I confessed. "Where do we go now? Second period? I've got to hurry if—"

"Hey, you're a Gold now," he said, grinning at me. "You can use any staircase you like."

There was a lot of laughter and catcalls and hooting in the halls this time; some of the new Golds—the light blondes—were wearing their circles on their foreheads like a badge, swaggering around as though they owned the place. I got a picture of that, and of a guy going up the front staircase giving the finger to one of the new Whites down below.

Lori and Leslie and I walked to the cafeteria together, and I got the first bacon cheeseburger I'd had all week, while Lori had to wait at the back of the line. Leslie and I tried to let her get in front of us, but the other new Golds screeched and protested, and she immediately cut out.

"What are you trying to do, Alice?" someone yelled. "She had it good all week. Let *her* get a taste of what we went through."

I faced forward again and felt myself blush. This was crazy! It was also crazy that I'd passed Elizabeth and Gwen in the line and hadn't spoken to them. I told myself it was because I was talking to Lori and Leslie at the time, but deep down I suspected that any other day I would have stopped to talk. I was "getting even," and doing exactly what I had accused them of doing all week.

Outside, Pamela was having lunch again with the Bikers. She had come in and gotten a tray of cheeseburgers for all of them and was handing them out flirtatiously, wearing the tightest jeans I'd seen on her yet. Even though she was a Gold now, she seemed to take delight in thumbing her nose at the rules. I took a picture from the hall window, but I wasn't going to turn it over to the school paper. I wanted to give it to Pamela sometime when we were alone to show her exactly how she looked.

Things got even worse that afternoon. Somebody claimed he was pushed away from the water cooler, and the Bikers developed a sign—a combination "heil" sign and a slash mark across the throat—that they used to greet each other and shock everybody else, I guess. Someone was playing a boom box in the rest room, one of the new Golds, I suppose.

The last period of the day was canceled, and Mr.

Ormand announced an assembly. Attendance would be taken at the door.

"Students," Mr. Ormand said, "we have held an experiment at this school we've never tried before. We didn't know exactly what we were starting with, or what we would have when we finished, so I think it's a credit to all of you that you were willing to go along with this, to explore both sides of this thing called 'prejudice,' and get some idea of how we fall into the patterns that we do—because we have all, this past week, had a taste of power and a taste of prejudice. We had a look at how we ourselves behaved in each situation."

Then he went on to say that this, the final day of the experiment, would be a tribute to the resiliency of the human spirit, our ability to survive adversity, our capacity for empathy, and our determination to change.

"As a testament to our belief in the Bill of Rights and equal treatment for all people," he said, "I invite all students to stand together to sing our school song and then, row by row, if you so wish, to come down to the center of the gym and drop your circles into the trash barrel. Here, in this school, we are all equal."

Several members of the school band started playing the school song. We stood up and began singing, and across the gym I saw some of the students link arms and do the Big Sway, as we call it. It spread from one set of bleachers to the next, until we were all arm in arm, we were all swaying, while row by row, students went down to throw out their circles before they walked silently out of the gym to get their jackets and catch their buses. It was one of the most solemn ceremonies I can remember: dropping our circles in the trash container, as though it could—*hoping* it could—rid us of prejudice, make us whole again. There was a lump in my throat as big as a lemon.

When Elizabeth came out, I saw tears in her eyes, and realized there were tears in mine too. Some of the kids were giving each other high fives, but we all noticed how *quiet* it was when we went outside to the bus. No hooting or laughing. Everyone seemed thoughtful. I felt fresh and new and cleansed, and when Gwen stopped and gave me a hug as she went by, she said she felt just like she did after she attended a church revival service once with her grandmother.

Elizabeth and I got on the bus together and sat side by side, the first time we'd done that all week. It was a brand-new start. A brave new world.

And then I realized that Pamela was missing.

5

Neck to Knees

"Where's Pamela?" I asked, looking around.

"Wasn't she at the assembly?" Patrick called.

"She wasn't with us. I haven't seen her since lunch." I looked at Elizabeth. "Have you?"

She shook her head.

"The blonde girl with the short hair, you mean?" a guy said. "I saw her leaving with the Bikers after lunch. I think she skipped."

Elizabeth and I both shot up out of our seats.

"She skipped school?" I cried. "The assembly and everything?"

"With the *Bikers*?" Elizabeth squeaked.

The boy looked chagrined. "Yeah. I *guess* she skipped. I mean, I saw them leave. She was sitting sideways on the bar of a guy's bike."

I sank down in the seat again, and Patrick came forward and sat down across from us.

"She's probably okay. I know some of those

guys," he said. "They're not too bad."

"'Not too bad' translated means 'not too good,' either," I told him. I wasn't reassured.

"So what did you think of CRW?" he asked me.

"I didn't think an experiment could make me feel so much like an outsider, but it did," I told him.

"Brian heard from Sorringer that a reporter's writing it up for the *Washington Post*," Patrick said. "They had a photographer there today, you know."

"We'll be famous," I said dryly. It *had* been an interesting experiment, but I was worried about Pamela. When Patrick got off at his stop, Elizabeth and I went into a huddle.

"What do you think we should do?" I asked.

"I think we should go over there and sit on her front steps waiting for her when she gets home," Elizabeth said.

We both knew that with her mom living in an apartment and her dad at work, Pamela had no one waiting for her, no one who knew where she was.

"We've got to be there for her," Elizabeth said determinedly, and I agreed.

I dropped my backpack off at my house, Elizabeth stopped off at hers, and then we set out for Pamela's. Just as we thought, she wasn't home.

We sat down on her front steps and stared out at the street.

"Today," said Elizabeth, "was one of the most . . . most moving days of my life. This past week has been so weird, Alice!"

"I know," I said.

"I mean, I didn't know how something as stupid as a dumb circle could *change* me so much."

"Me either."

We sat quietly for a while, not saying anything. Then Elizabeth said, "What if . . . what if the week changed Pamela *too* much?"

"Changed her how?"

"What if she decided that if she's going to be treated like dirt, it doesn't matter what she does? She never skipped school before."

"I know. She never went off with the Bikers, either," I said.

"What if . . . she felt more kinds of feelings than we know about, Alice?"

"What do you mean?"

"What if she rode off with the Bleached Bike Boys and they took her to their den?"

"Den?"

"Their hideout."

"*Hideout?*"

"Well, their hangout, then. Wherever it is they do what they do."

"They ride bikes, Elizabeth. They probably ride on the street."

"Okay, then. What if they take her to a back-street somewhere and . . . and rape her?"

"Don't *say* that, Elizabeth! I'm worried enough about her already."

"So am I. But what if they do?"

I was miserable. "I guess we won't know till she gets here," I said.

"You don't think we ought to call the police?"

"And tell them what? That a friend of ours is riding around somewhere on a bike? She went willingly, didn't she? Nobody reported them carrying her off kicking and screaming."

"But what if she *does* get raped, Alice, and doesn't tell anybody?"

I hugged my knees and tried not to think about it, but Elizabeth went barreling on.

"What if she gets pregnant and stays inside all summer and never goes over to Mark's pool and goes around in baggy clothes till September, and then she keeps skipping gym? And around Christmas, when everyone else is singing carols, what if Pamela goes out in the garage and has a baby in the backseat of her dad's Chevrolet, and it's a little boy, only she can't stand the thought that he might grow up to be a rapist too like his father, so she—"

"Elizabeth, shut up," I said.

"But she'd go to prison for *murder,* Alice! You and I would have to go visit her every Sunday and take her fruit, and—"

At that very moment we saw Pamela coming up the street, her backpack hanging from one shoulder, her jacket unbuttoned, her hair sort of wild.

"Pamela?" we said together when she reached the gate.

Pamela stared at us, then unlatched the gate. "What are *you* guys doing here?" she asked.

"Where have you been?" Elizabeth demanded.

"We were worried about you!" I told her.

"Okay, so I skipped, but it's not a felony," Pamela said. "You thought I met up with the Boston Strangler or something?"

"We didn't know *what* might have happened to you. An accident or something," I said.

"We thought you were raped," said Elizabeth.

"*What?*" Pamela cried.

"You've never skipped school before, Pamela," I told her.

"And you've never hung around the Bikers, either," said Elizabeth.

Pamela put her key in the lock, and we followed her inside.

"Well, for your information," she said, "I'm just fine. We went to John's house and listened to a new CD and kidded around, and then went out for pizza." She dropped her backpack on the couch. "Anyone want a diet Coke?"

Elizabeth didn't budge. "What do you mean, 'kidded around'?" she asked.

"Joked! Laughed! Cut up! Don't look at me that way, Elizabeth," Pamela said, but I noticed she was avoiding our eyes. "Nothing happened that wasn't by mutual consent."

"I guess that's what's worrying us, Pamela," I said quietly.

She still didn't look at me. "Well, don't!" she snapped. "I can take care of myself."

"Pamela, just tell me one thing," said Elizabeth. "Are you still a virgin?"

"*What?*" cried Pamela. "What *is* this? The Spanish Inquisition? Do I have to tell you every time a guy touches me?"

"They touched you? Where?" Elizabeth wanted to know.

"For Pete's sake! None of your business!" Pamela said.

All the closeness and friendship I'd felt during assembly that afternoon seemed to evaporate like steam on a mirror. Pamela and Elizabeth and I had been through so much together, ever since sixth grade. We'd told each other *every*thing, practically. And now I realized that where boys were concerned, we'd probably start holding stuff back. Keeping secrets. Sharing things with our boyfriends instead. Maybe this was normal, the way things were supposed to be, but I didn't think I liked it.

Elizabeth sat as stiff as a broom on the sofa, arms at her sides. I think we both felt awkward, like we were in the presence of a *woman,* maybe, and we didn't know what to say.

"Oh, for crying out loud!" Pamela said finally. "One of the guys slipped his hands under my sweater, that's all." And then, looking right at Elizabeth, she added, "Yes, he touched my breasts. He got a three-second feel through my bra, and then I pushed him away, okay?"

We still didn't say anything. I don't know what Elizabeth was thinking, but I was remembering the time in Patrick's basement when he was giving me a drum lesson. How he'd sat close behind me, holding me in his arms. He didn't touch my breasts—he almost did—but I'll have to admit I sort of wanted him to. I mean, that's what sex is all about, isn't it? You're *supposed* to want to caress each other. It's *supposed* to feel good. It's natural. It's normal. So when are you supposed to stop saying no and start saying yes?

Elizabeth answered for me. "You're supposed to do that after you're married, Pamela. At *least* after you're engaged."

"Yeah? Tell that to my mom," Pamela said bitterly. "*She's* married, only she's doing it with someone else. And I'll bet she's letting him do a lot more than that."

I guess I acted on instinct. I went over, sat down by Pamela, and put my arms around her. "I'm glad you're back," I said. "I'm glad the week's over. We missed you."

I held her tight, like I'd hold a little sister, and the crazy, surprising thing was, she started crying, very quietly. I could feel a tear on my neck. At the same time, though, I think she was embarrassed about it.

"I am just so mad at my mother!" she said, fumbling for a tissue finally.

"Well, don't take it out on yourself," I said. "You're too wonderful, Pamela, to throw yourself away on somebody who doesn't deserve you."

"Who says I was throwing myself away?" she asked, sniffling a little.

"All I know is you can do a lot better than those bleached-blond Bikers who make a point of looking funky—like it's the only thing they've got going for them," I said.

Then Elizabeth got into the act. "You know that time we went to Chicago on the train, the three of us, and that man came in your compartment and kissed you and touched your breasts, Pamela?"

she said. "I think that started all this. I think it set up cravings in you that you just can't control."

We stared at her.

"The thing is, Pamela," she continued, "if you let a boy get to first base, he'll try to get to second, and if he gets to second, he'll steal third, and . . ."

"Ye gods, Elizabeth, I'm not playing baseball, I'm making out!" Pamela said. "And you know what? It feels good! People act so surprised when you say that. Like, boys make out because it feels good, and girls just do it to please the boys."

She got some diet Coke from the fridge and we put all the sofa cushions on the rug, then sprawled on the floor.

"You're right, you know," said Elizabeth. "At church, Sister Madeline never talks about how we might do something like that because we want to. She's never ever once said that it might be fun."

"Of course! How would she know, she's a nun!" I said.

Elizabeth sighed. "You know what I wish? I wish that we could just go to sleep some night and wake up married. Then we could do anything with our husbands that we wanted, and we wouldn't go to hell and we wouldn't have to confess anything to the priest, because it would all be legal."

We thought about that awhile. It certainly had its attractions.

"You wouldn't have to worry about *who* to marry," I said. "The decision would have been made already, and you could get on with your life."

"But think of all the fun you'd miss!" Pamela said mischievously. "The flirtation, the courtship, the first kiss, the first . . . well, whatever you do before you're married."

"Grope," said Elizabeth.

"What?" I asked.

"Grope. It's when a boy touches any part of you that your bathing suit is supposed to cover," Elizabeth informed us.

I could see Pamela's face beginning to crinkle a little around the eyes.

"That's what Sister Madeline told us," Elizabeth continued. "She said that's all we have to remember when we're out on a date. Never let the boy grope."

"Wow! I like that!" said Pamela. "That means he could caress your back, and the top of your leg along your inner thigh . . ." She faked a shiver.

"And how about those thong bathing suits, where both cheeks are open to the public?" I put in.

"Not *those* kinds of suits!" said Elizabeth.

"Maybe Sister Madeline needs to get to the beach more often and see what women are wearing," said Pamela.

"Maybe she should have said 'nothing between

the neck and the knees,'" said Elizabeth, thinking it over.

"From wrists to elbows on Mondays, Wednesdays, and Fridays only," joked Pamela.

"Feet and calves on Tuesdays, Thursdays, and Saturdays," I added.

"But nothing on Sunday!" said Elizabeth, and we all started to laugh.

Pamela was back, and it was like old times.

"You know what?" I said. "I'm just going to take it slow and easy and see what happens. But, like Carol told me, I'm going to make sure I know a guy really, really well, and like him an awful lot before I . . . uh . . ." I couldn't find the right word.

"Grope," said Elizabeth.

"Whatever," I told her.

6

April Showers

The *Washington Post* ran a feature story in the Metro section on CRW, but I didn't think their pictures were as good as Sam's. When our school newspaper came out with a two-page photo spread—mostly kids' faces reacting to one of the rules—four of the pictures were taken by Sam. Mine turned out only so-so.

"Great photos," I told him in Camera Club when it met after school the following Wednesday. Everyone was praising Sam.

He grinned, obviously pleased.

"You know how many shots I took in all? Thirty-six. Divided by four makes nine. Only one out of nine made it."

"Well, they didn't use any of mine," I said.

"Next time," he told me, and squeezed my arm.

"But you see picture possibilities in things that the rest of us probably wouldn't consider. And you'd have had to have split-second timing to get some of those, Sam."

"More like luck," he said, and went on over to help frame one of the enlargements for the school bulletin board.

I watched him kidding around with some of the other club members. In some ways he's like Patrick, and in some ways he's just the opposite. Patrick's tall, Sam's shorter. Patrick's lean, Sam's heavier—slightly muscular. Patrick has red hair, Sam's is dark. Patrick's more confident, I think; Sam's quieter. But they're both really nice. They both pay attention to me, listen to what I say. I felt like Miss Summers must feel, I guess: I had two guys I liked a lot.

Now that we'd all survived CRW, everybody's thoughts turned to the eighth-grade semi-formal, meaning that girls get to wear fancy dresses, but the guys just wear suits. Before, it was mostly couples who were already going together who started making plans, but now people were making dates, and every day we'd hear about another girl who'd been asked or a girl who had asked a guy.

I was going with Patrick, of course, and Elizabeth with Justin Collier. Mark and Brian both asked Pamela, but she turned them down. Elizabeth and I were afraid she'd go with one of the Bikers, but for kicks, she really did invite my old boyfriend from Takoma Park, Donald Sheavers. Maybe he'll grow up to be a nuclear physicist, I don't know, but he's not very smart as far as human relations go. Elizabeth and I were so glad that Pamela wasn't going with one of the bleached boys, though, that we told her she was welcome to ride with us.

The deal was that Justin's father would take us all in his van and Lester would pick us up afterward. Actually, Justin and Patrick wanted Donald Sheavers to go in with them and rent a limo for the evening, but Patrick's dad wouldn't hear of it. If anyone in the whole school could afford a limo it was Mr. Long, but he said that if a guy rented a limo for his eighth-grade semi-formal, he'd have to rent a yacht for his high school prom. And if he rented a yacht for the senior prom, he'd have to rent the Concorde for his wedding, because what else was left?

Anyway, it was good to be thinking about the semi-formal, with CRW behind us. Elizabeth said she thought everyone was kinder to each other since CRW. I wasn't sure of that, but I think we were a little more thoughtful, at least.

The first week of April, Miss Summers stayed after school a couple of hours each day to finish some work she had to do.

"Why don't you come by the house later and

have dinner here, Sylvia?" I heard Dad ask her over the phone. "I'm making shrimp and pasta. It's no trouble."

She must have said yes because Dad hummed as he made dinner that night, and I set the table with extra care, trying not to make a big deal of it. I knew that if Miss Summers eventually chose Mr. Sorringer over Dad, it would be hard enough for him without me getting upset over it too.

At first I thought she wasn't coming. She'd told Dad she'd probably be here by six forty-five, but at five of seven she still hadn't shown, and Lester was hanging around the kitchen, his stomach growling.

"You can go ahead and eat, Les," Dad said. "I've got the pasta warming in the oven."

"That's okay," Lester said. "I can wait."

Seven came, then five after. Dad wordlessly took out the pasta and mixed it with sauce. Then we heard a car door slam, footsteps on the porch, and Dad's face lit up like a flashlight.

"I'm so sorry!" Miss Summers said, slipping off her sweater. "I was blocks away from the school when I realized I'd left some papers behind that had to be mailed off to England, and I had to go all the way back. I hoped you'd start without me."

"If I'd gotten a head start, there wouldn't be any left," Lester joked.

"You're worth the wait, Sylvia," Dad said. "Please sit down."

Miss Summers has light brown hair and blue eyes. She's beautiful and smart and exactly the right size and shape for my father. They look great together. What Dad calls her, though, is "serene." She's easy to get along with, he says. Interesting to talk to. A good listener. A good friend.

"I see you survived CRW," she said to me, unfolding her napkin and spreading it on her lap. She was wearing an olive green knit dress with a green and gold scarf at the neck. Her nails were polished a rich clay color.

"It was okay, but I'm glad it's over," I told her. "One more day, and I don't know what would have happened. Tempers were really hot on Friday."

"I know. There was a sign over the copier in the teachers' lounge saying that the group A teachers got to use it first. If any A teacher wanted something copied, any B or C had to let her go first. We joked about it, but by Friday, the brunettes were really getting ugly looks. I had an orange circle, so I was sort of in-between."

"Me too," I said. "The worst of both worlds."

"Well, turnaround day on Friday must have been something!" said Lester. "All the Had-Nots attacking the Hads."

Miss Summers laughed. "Actually, we were quite civilized about it. Though Mr. Ormand, who chose to be in the C group even though he's bald, did admit that one more day without a bacon cheeseburger would probably have put him over the edge." She took a bite of shrimp. "Oh, Ben, this is delicious!"

"I'm glad you came by," he told her, and I think they touched hands under the table.

"How are things going with you, Les?" she asked, lifting her coffee to her lips and looking at Lester with her blue, blue eyes. "How's the philosophy major?"

"I've barely gotten my feet wet," Les told her. "This semester we're studying the Socratic method, but it's still introductory. I'm looking forward to the seminars in graduate school."

"And after your master's degree?" she asked.

Lester made his usual joke: "I'll sit on a mountaintop and reveal the meaning of life."

"His secret of life is to stay in school as long as possible and live off his old man," Dad said, and we all laughed.

"What about you, Sylvia?" Lester asked. "You leave in June, don't you? You must be pretty excited."

"I am. Though in a way, I hate to leave. But I've found a renter for my house for a year who says she'll take good care of my flowers. If I don't go now when I've got the chance, I probably never would, so I've talked myself into it," Miss Summers said.

We all knew that she was going to England for a year as an exchange teacher so she could decide between Dad and Jim Sorringer. But we pretended it was just travel that interested her.

"I'm trying to get Ben to come over and visit me while I'm there," she added.

I put down my fork and looked at Dad. I could tell that Lester had stopped chewing too. If she was going to England to be by herself and think, and then she wanted Dad there, didn't that mean that . . . ?

"You're going, of course," Lester said to Dad.

"Well, I'm taking it under consideration," Dad said. "Janice would have to take over the store, and I'd be leaving you two alone for a week or so."

"*Go,* Dad!" I said. "You've never been to England. Janice Sherman is perfectly capable of running the place. That's what assistant managers are for. You've *got* to go!"

"That's what I told him," Miss Summers said. "I think he'd enjoy it."

"You know I would," Dad told her, smiling. "I'm working on it."

"You won't have to worry about a thing here,"

Les said. "If Al gets out of line, I'll just chain her in the cellar till you get back. No problem at all."

After dinner Les went bowling with some of his buddies, and Miss Summers absolutely insisted on doing the dishes. I started to protest that I'd do them, but figured it was a way for her and Dad to be alone, so I took my books up to my room to study.

I worked for about an hour, then noticed it had been raining lightly—an April shower. With my window open, I could smell the sweet scent of damp earth and new grass. I stretched and wondered when it was safe to go back downstairs. I hadn't heard Miss Summers's car leave, but I didn't hear any dishes rattling in the kitchen, either.

I turned off my light and went over to the window. Sitting down on the floor, I rested my arms on the sill and drank in the spring perfume. The gentle raindrops sounded like tiny drummers in the rain gutter overhead. I was watching a couple far down the block moving past the street lamp and into the shadows of the trees, then emerging again, stopping to kiss. As they came closer, I realized it was Dad and Miss Summers, and they didn't have an umbrella. I'll bet they didn't even know it was raining.

I don't know why, but I cried. I was thinking of

my mom, whom I hardly even remembered. I wished I had at least one memory of Dad kissing her.

We were starting to think about dresses for the semi-formal. I'd be wearing the jade green brides-maid's dress, of course, that I'd worn for Crystal's wedding. And shortly after Justin Collier had asked Elizabeth to go to the dance with him, Elizabeth and her mom went shopping and bought an off-the-shoulder pink satin dress with a slim skirt. Elizabeth held it up against her for Pamela and me to see, and it looked like a rose against her creamy skin. Elizabeth has the most beautiful skin of any girl I've ever known.

Pamela was the only one of us who didn't have a dress. Her father said it was her mom's job to help her choose one, but Mrs. Jones was off some-where with her NordicTrack instructor, so once again Pamela was out in left field.

Elizabeth and I said we'd go shopping with her, but we were a little worried about the kind of dress she might choose, the way she'd been act-ing lately. I knew she liked Lester, though, and would probably listen to him, and I tried to figure out a way to get him to come with us.

When he got home from bowling, I made some popcorn and took it up to his room. "Want some?" I said, and set the bowl on his desk.

"Thanks. Now if you'd bring me a beer . . . ," he said.

"We don't have any beer, Lester."

"Well, I'll make do," he said, and settled back on his bed with a philosophy book in his lap.

"Lester," I said, "what would you say if I told you that someone needs you in a very special way?"

Lester slowly lowered the book. "Needs me how? Who've you been talking to, Al? Marilyn? Not *Crystal*?"

"It's one of my friends, Lester."

"Oh, no! The last time somebody 'needed' me, it was Elizabeth who'd never seen a naked man."

I grinned, remembering how I'd tried to get Lester to buy a magazine for her—one of those magazines of hunks.

"It's not that," I said. "It's just that Pamela's parents are fighting, and her mom's off with her NordicTrack instructor, and her dad says it's her mom's duty to help her buy a dress, but . . ."

"So what am *I* supposed to do? Shoot the guy on the NordicTrack?"

"Take Pamela shopping."

"Are you totally out of your mind?"

"Elizabeth and I will go with you, but Pamela's been sort of wild lately, and we're afraid she'll buy a dress that's embarrassing or something. She'd listen to you, though."

"I don't know anything about dresses."

"You'd know if it was indecent," I told him.

"I'd rather have a root canal," said Lester.

"When was the last time you did something really selfless and noble and good and true?" I said.

"It'll cost you, kid."

"How much?"

"If Crystal calls, you have to get rid of her for me."

"Lie?"

"Be creative. I don't want to be involved in her squabbles with Peter."

"Okay. Deal. Wheaton Plaza on Saturday?"

Lester sighed. "I'll meet you there after I get off work at Maytag. I'll give you from three to five, but at five o'clock, I walk."

On Saturday, I put in my three hours at the Melody Inn, and was able to avoid Marilyn. I talked a few minutes with Janice Sherman, but Dad asked me to help put up shelves in the store basement for supplies, so all I said to Marilyn was hello and good-bye. I didn't know if she was still crying over Les, but I didn't want to be around if she was.

Lester came to Wheaton Plaza as promised, and we explained that there were five stores we wanted to visit even if Pamela didn't try anything on. She didn't want to buy a dress only to find out that there was a better one right next door. So we walked on ahead, and Lester followed at a safe distance.

"Like a secret service agent," Pamela giggled.

The first store didn't have any dresses that Pamela liked, so we headed for the next one and got waylaid at an accessory shop looking at earrings.

"Nope! Nix! Move on, ladies. You buy a dress and I go home. That was the bargain," Lester called from the doorway. The customers turned to stare at us, but Pamela only giggled. She loved having Les along.

We lost him momentarily, however, when we passed Victoria's Secret, because there was a mannequin in the window wearing black bikini panties, a black garter belt, white stockings, and heels, and on top, nothing but a black tuxedo jacket, unbuttoned, of course.

"Nope! Nix! Move on, Lester," Elizabeth called, and I believe he actually blushed a little as he moved up behind us and we set out for Penney's.

In the junior department, Lester leaned against a pillar with his hands in his pockets while we slid the dresses along the rack, checking each one.

Pamela found a black dress made of fake

leather and held it up for Lester to see.

"Get real," he said.

Then we saw a royal blue dress that was nice—long and sleek—with a slit almost up to the panty line. The three of us went in the dressing room while Pamela tried it on. It wrinkled a little at the waist—they didn't have it in size six—but we persuaded her to come out and show it to Lester anyway. He was chewing gum and eyeing a customer over in the lingerie section. When he turned back again, there was Pamela, smiling at him.

I think he swallowed his gum. "Go put your clothes on," he said.

"*Les*-ter!" I chided.

"It's too long waisted," he argued. "It wrinkles. You can do better than that, Pamela."

That convinced us, so Pamela got dressed again, and we tried two other stores and didn't find anything. Then we walked to Hecht's at the other end. There were two dresses that looked right for Pamela, and the salesclerk, a tall blonde, hung them outside a corner dressing room with a three-way mirror and left us to ourselves.

Pamela put on the deep purple one first, something like the blue dress, but cut low in back, with a halter top.

"Oh, Pamela!" I said when I saw her in it. "It's perfect!"

"It's a little low in back," said Elizabeth. "A boy could put his hand inside if he wanted."

We both looked at Elizabeth.

"She's going with Donald *Sheavers*!" I reminded her. "She'd have to give him directions."

"Go show Lester," Elizabeth said.

Pamela opened the dressing room door. Lester was sitting on a folding chair. He'd found a newspaper and was reading the sports section.

"Lester!" Pamela called, walking toward him like a model, one leg out in front of the other, and she did a pivot right in front of him, one hand on her hip.

"Ye gods!" said Lester when he saw the back of the dress. Or rather, the back of Pamela where there wasn't any dress.

"I think it's perfect," I told him.

"Too tight," said Lester.

"It's not, Les! That's the way it's supposed to fit!" Pamela argued.

"It's indecent," he said. "Look at the back!"

"See?" said Elizabeth triumphantly.

We went back to the dressing room, and I began to wish I hadn't brought my brother. I didn't think he'd be this much of a prude. He still thought of us as children.

"Put on the red one," I said to Pamela, pointing to the dress with the short swishy skirt and the low, low neckline.

She did, and even I decided she'd set off a fire alarm. "Tell Lester it's between this and the purple."

The way Pamela was looking at herself in the mirror, I was afraid she'd choose this one. It was Pamela, all right—the way she'd been behaving lately, anyway. I began to wish I hadn't come. I didn't want to be responsible.

"Go show Lester," was all Elizabeth could muster.

Pamela flounced out of the dressing room and stood in front of Lester, her breasts puffing out at the neckline.

He blinked. I think he could tell that Pamela liked this one too.

"It'd be great for Halloween," he said. "Great if you want to look like a hooker. But if you want to look sexy yet subtle, exciting but sophisticated, choose the purple, Pamela."

"Okay," she said, much to our relief, and went back in the dressing room.

There, however, we discovered a little plastic bag with foam rubber cups in it that came with the red dress. When we investigated, we discovered that there were pouches in the bosom of the dress, and if we inserted the foam rubber, it would push Pamela's breasts up even farther.

We couldn't resist. I thrust my hand down one

side of the neckline to insert the foam rubber, and Elizabeth thrust her hand down into the neckline on the other side. When Pamela stood up straight, though, and thrust out her chest, one of the foam pads popped out like popcorn, and we shrieked with laughter.

Elizabeth tried again, and this time, because the dress was so tight, the pouch pushed Pamela's breast up so high that a nipple popped up over the top. We screamed again.

"Donald would pass out," Pamela said, wiping her eyes.

"He wouldn't even know what it was," I said, and we howled some more.

Then we heard Lester's voice outside the dressing room.

". . . try to overlook a lot," he was saying. "I'm acting custodian for the day."

We hushed.

"What's the matter with them?" The saleswoman's voice.

"Developmental problems, you know."

"Oh. They seemed perfectly normal. . . ." the clerk said.

"Yeah, they'll fool you every time," said Lester.

7

Lori Haynes

I spent most of April, it seemed, playing with Elizabeth's little brother, Nathan, who's almost seven months old now, and really cute. He's just beginning to cry when she hands him to strangers, and I feel pretty flattered that he'll let me carry him around.

Pamela and I play peekaboo with him a lot. Once, up in his room, Pamela got down on the floor on one side of his crib and I got down on the other, and we kept popping up—first one of us on one side, then the other—and saying, "Boo!" and he got so excited he just crowed. Screamed, almost, then giggled. When you look at a little baby like that, you realize that if he thinks *this* is exciting, wait till he rides his first Ferris wheel! Steers his first bike! Tries out a pair of RollerBlades or goes down a hill on a sled. All the stuff this little kid has waiting for him! And I think how, if I'm a parent, it's up to me to protect this new little life so he'll grow up to *have* a future.

"Is it scary?" I asked Mrs. Price as I helped her get a shirt over Nathan's head, which must be something like trying to put a sweater on an octopus.

"Scary?"

"Knowing that you're responsible for him till he's eighteen years old. Maybe more," I said.

She laughed. "With your first one, you're extra cautious, I think. You always check to make sure he's still breathing. But after a while you relax a little and the baby relaxes, and, of course, you get a lot of help. There are always people eager to tell you how to raise a child. Mostly, you just have to trust yourself."

Interesting, I thought, how often I hear, "Trust yourself." Trust yourself that you're smart enough to get through algebra. Trust yourself to act natural with a boy. Trust yourself that you'll choose the right career. Sort of makes you feel like everyone else has a more grown-up self than you do.

"What philosopher was it who said, 'Trust yourself'?" I asked Lester. He was standing at his mirror putting on a tie.

"Emerson. 'Trust thyself. Every heart vibrates to that inner string.' Or something like that."

"Whatever. Do you trust yourself?"

"Most of the time."

"Do you know, then, why you keep turning down wonderful girls like Marilyn and Crystal?"

"Is this conversation going somewhere?"

"I'm just asking, Lester, why you keep letting wonderful women get away. I think it's because you're afraid that if you really fall for a nice girl, she might die, like Mom did, and you can't stand the possibility of being abandoned twice."

"Who are you? Sigmund Freud?"

"I read it in a magazine at the dentist's. This woman wrote that her nephew never dated nice girls since his mother died; he always dated floozies."

"*Floozies?* How old was that magazine? The nineteen twenties?"

"I *worry* about you, Lester! All these girls are madly in love with you, and—"

"There were two, to be exact."

"And you let them get away."

"One fell in love with someone else, remember."

"But Crystal still loves you, and you know it."

"Well, I'm flattered," Lester said, "but I don't go out with married women. Which is why, if you re-call, you promised to fend off any more phone calls from Crystal, if there are any."

"I'll remember," I told him. I realized he'd never worn a tie to Maytag before. "Where are *you* going?" I asked.

"New job. Shoe store, ten to five on Saturdays, plus Tuesday and Thursday evenings. Need some extra money." He slipped his arms in his suit coat. "See you, kid," he said, and clattered downstairs.

I stood at the window as Lester got in his car and drove away. Everything seemed to be changing lately. People made changes in their lives without even telling me about them. But it was nothing like I felt when I saw Pamela going up the steps of Elizabeth's house across the street. Nobody said anything to me about going to Elizabeth's! I turned and stared at the phone in the hallway, waiting for it to ring. It didn't.

I slid down on the floor against the wall and cried. Just because I didn't like to talk about dresses and makeup all the time. Just because I didn't like to fool around with my hair. They could have invited me anyway, couldn't they? They could at least have let me refuse!

"I saw you at Elizabeth's this morning," I said to Pamela later when she called.

"Oh, yeah," she said. "We were trying on earrings. We didn't think you'd be interested."

Gwen and Lori had both been extra nice to me since CRW. Maybe they were feeling a little guilty because they'd been part of the A group, with all its perks.

"Here," said Gwen, dropping a paper on my desk during homeroom the following week. "I picked up an application for candy striper at Suburban Hospital this summer and got an extra one for you, if you're interested."

"I am!" I said. "Thanks."

Lori made it a point to sit by me in biology when she got the chance, and we always walked to and from the gym together. *She'd be a lot more attractive if she'd stand up straight,* I thought, but she hunches over her books when she walks as though she's trying to be as short as everyone else. If tall girls only knew how they *looked* when they did that, but I guess none of us want to be told how we really look.

She's right across from me in the locker room, and Lori's got a nice shape, even though she doesn't have much bosom. I guess you're not supposed to look at each other's bodies in the locker room, not so it's noticeable, anyway, but of course we all do. We're comparing ourselves with everyone else. The seventh-graders frankly stare. I stared too in seventh grade, because I'd never seen so many naked girls all at one time, but in eighth grade we don't pay that much attention anymore. I caught Lori looking at me, though. I guess if you're tall and feel different from other girls, you always want to see how you measure up.

I'll bet boys peek at each other all the time.

It's really amazing how different girls' bodies are. No two are the same. Some have fine silky hair over their arms and thighs and abdomens; some have navels that poke out, some have belly buttons that tuck in; some have big nipples, small nipples, big buttocks, no buttocks—every single part of a woman is different in some way, which means that every single one of us is normal. You might think, *Nobody else has a part that looks like mine,* but if you look long enough you'll find hundreds. Thousands. Millions, I'll bet. Pamela says the "ideal" figure is the way models look, and I say if American girls all looked as skinny as models, other countries would be sending their corn and wheat to *us*!

Lori and I were talking about our brothers in gym. We'd just come out of the shower, and I told her how Lester goes around the house in his Mickey Mouse shorts. She laughed.

"I've got *two* brothers," she said, drying the back of her neck.

"Older or younger?"

"Older, like yours."

"Is your mom living?" I asked, and then, when she looked at me sort of weird, I realized that most people don't go around asking that. You just assume that their mothers are there, unless they've run off with NordicTrack instructors or something.

"Of course," said Lori. Then she said, "Why don't you come over Friday and meet my family? Spend the night?"

"Sure," I said. "Except that I work in my dad's store over on Georgia Avenue on Saturday mornings."

"Mom will drive you," she said.

So I agreed to go home on the bus with her on Friday.

Why is it that as soon as you do something with a new girlfriend, your best friends get upset? Elizabeth and Pamela had been doing all sorts of things without me, but as soon as *I* did something different, I heard about it.

"You're going to Lori Haynes's?" Pamela said when I mentioned it to her.

"Yeah. She asked me. She's got brothers too. She seems nice."

Pamela and Elizabeth grew quiet.

"We've always done stuff together on weekends, Alice," Elizabeth said. "And she didn't invite *us*."

"Hey, we're not Siamese triplets," I told her, trying to joke about it. "We can still do something on Saturday. You guys do things sometimes without me!"

The weird thing was, I got sort of the same reaction from Dad.

"What's her last name?" he asked.

"Haynes."

"Ever meet her parents? What does her dad do?"

I was beginning to get ticked off. "I don't know. You want to call the FBI and check them out?" I snapped.

"Honey, I just don't like the idea of you sleeping in a home where there's a father I don't know anything about."

I went to the phone and called Lori. I told her my father was insane, and that somehow we had to convince him that her dad wasn't an ax murderer or a rapist. She laughed. "I'll have my mom call your dad," she said, and ten minutes later, the phone rang.

I don't know what Mrs. Haynes said, but I could see Dad beginning to relax, and when he hung up, he said, "That was Lori's mother. She assures me you'll be well taken care of, and I feel I know the family a little better. You can go, Al, but call me if you ever feel uncomfortable somewhere."

Ha! If I called Dad every time I felt "uncomfortable," I'd have to wear a walkie-talkie. I'd have called him the time Patrick took me to his parents' country club for dinner. I'd have called him from Mrs. Plotkin's room back in sixth grade, and from Mark Stedmeister's swimming pool. From the doctor's, the lingerie shower for Crystal, and from the broom closet at school on Halloween. Dad has no idea that I spend 95 percent of my life feeling "uncomfortable."

"Uncomfortable, or in danger of my life?" I asked.

"Life, limb, or moral values," said Dad, which meant that for ordinary, common, garden-variety embarrassments, I was on my own.

Lori seemed really glad to have me. On the bus to her house—she lives out in Glenmont near Wheaton Plaza—she stretched out one leg alongside mine, and I noticed how really long it was. I felt like a shrimp next to her.

"When did you start school?" I asked her. "I don't remember you here last year."

"No one remembers me," she said ruefully, pulling her dark bangs down over her face like she was trying to hide. "I was here, but I'm pretty shy, I guess. I got my growth spurt around December of seventh grade, and shot up like a beanstalk. I honestly think some kids thought I was a different person. Didn't even recognize me when I came back last fall."

Her house is a Cape Cod, with one big room on the second floor. Her mom's always been a housewife, Lori said, and her dad's an engineer. He didn't say much, but her mom was friendly.

She made taco salad for dinner, which was great. Her brothers seemed *really* shy. They're sixteen and seventeen, and have rooms in the basement, so Lori and I had the whole upper floor to ourselves. There were twin beds and a dresser at one end, and a foam rubber sofa and hassock and TV at the other—sort of like her own little apartment.

"Lori, this is great!" I told her. "You could have parties up here and everything!"

"I guess," she said, pleased that I liked it. "One of the perks of being the only girl in the family, I guess."

We took off our shoes and sat on her sofa, our feet sharing the hassock, and looked through some screamingly funny books Lori had showing baby pictures of famous people. You were supposed to match the baby pictures with the right people. Some of the kids were picking their noses or pulling up their pants, and we'd yelp with laughter.

Then Lori got out a photograph album of her own, pictures of herself when she was small, and we laughed some more. I told her finally about Mom, and she didn't say anything at first. Then she just rubbed one of her feet gently against mine and said, "I'm really sorry, Alice."

"Thanks," I said. And that was all.

Her dad brought up some popcorn and went

right down again, and I had to smile when I thought how my dad was probably at home still worrying about whether Mr. Haynes or one of his sons was going to molest me. I thought about Nathan again too, and how much worrying Mrs. Price will do about him. There sure must be a lot to worry about when you're a parent!

"Want me to tell your future?" Lori asked after we'd finished the popcorn and were watching some stupid movie on TV, the sound turned so low it was practically off because it was so stupid.

I laughed. "Sure. As long as it's good."

"No. Really. I read a book on it once. All about life lines and stuff."

"Okay."

She took my hand and placed it palm side up in hers, and explained about what it meant if certain lines met or intersected or passed by each other entirely. I tried not to laugh, but it really tickled for some reason, the way she was running her finger along my palm. It wasn't very helpful—the fortune was so general it could have been anybody's—but the thing was, when she finished, she didn't let go of my hand. I'd just dropped it down between us, but she still had hold of it.

She's lonely, I thought. *Maybe tall, shy girls are just naturally lonely.*

I was feeling a little awkward, though, and I guess she was too, because she looked down at our hands, lifting my fingers up one at a time with her own, then letting them drop back down again, and then she said, "I really like you, Alice."

"I really like you too," I said. "I'm glad you asked me over."

"Are you?" she said.

"Sure. I've been trying to broaden myself this year. Meet new people."

"That's not what I meant," said Lori.

And finally I figured out what this was all about. My first thought was not to call Dad and ask him to come and get me. It wasn't to pull away from her, either, although I did remove my hand from hers and put it in my lap. I just wanted to sit there and listen to how she felt.

"Well," she joked. "You passed the first test. You didn't run screaming from the room."

"Why should I?" I said, and then I was sorry, because I could tell she thought maybe I liked her in that way too.

She glanced at me sideways. "You know what I mean, don't you?"

"That you like girls better than boys? Romantically, I mean?"

She took a deep breath and let it out. "Yeah, I think so," she said, without looking at me.

"Well, I like boys best—in a romantic way, I mean."

Lori tipped her head back and sat like that for several seconds. "Oh, gosh," she said, and slapped her forehead with the palm of her hand. "I came on too strong, didn't I? I shouldn't have hurried you."

"Lori, it wouldn't have made any difference if you'd taken a year to tell me this. I like you a lot, but I could never fall in love with you. Not like that. We're just different, that's all."

"You were always so nice to me. I guess I hoped."

"I'm really sorry."

We were both quiet for so long it was embarrassing.

"Do you want me to go home?" I asked finally.

"No, of course not," she said quickly. "Mom would ask why, and . . ."

"She doesn't know?"

"Hardly anyone does."

"We could say I got sick."

"No. Really. I want you to stay. We can at least talk, can't we?"

"Sure. Why not? I'm curious about why . . . Well, I just don't have the same feelings that you do. What made you think I did?"

"Nothing much. You smiled at me, that's all. You were always nice."

"But you must have heard I've been going with Patrick Long."

"That doesn't necessarily mean anything. I've heard of girls who went with boys first before they realized they were gay."

"Is that what you call it?"

"Well, lesbian. There. I've said it."

"Are you really sure? I mean, it's not as though you've felt this way for twenty years."

"Well, I've never had a girlfriend before, but I'd like to."

"Why *won't* you tell your folks?"

"I don't know. I'll have to eventually, I guess. Maybe I just want them to figure it out for themselves. I mean, I'm their only daughter. Mom's always buying me stuff with lace on it that makes me look like Goldilocks or something. A Cinderella doll when I was little. After two boys, she finally got a girl, but not the girl she wanted."

I wished I knew what to say to Lori. I tried to imagine what my own mother would say if I told her I was a lesbian, but I didn't ever know my own mother, so I can't imagine it. All I can imagine is my *ideal* mother. Or what my old sixth-grade teacher, Mrs. Plotkin, might say. Even Miss Summers.

"I'll bet she loves you for a lot more than you think," I said. "Not just because you're a girl."

"Maybe. But my dad . . . gosh, it would kill him."

"I doubt it. He looks pretty strong to me."

"My brothers probably wouldn't even speak to me."

"Lori, how do you know all this? I think the more you keep it from them, the worse you imagine things would be."

She shook her head. "I've read stories of what other girls go through when they tell."

"Well, you know what I think? I think your folks will get used to it in time. Your brothers too."

"They've had all this time since I was six years old. That's the soonest I began to think I was different—the soonest I can remember, anyway. Whenever Mom took me to a toy store, I went right to the boys' stuff. I always wanted cowboy things for Christmas. I wouldn't play with the Barbies." Lori laughed a little. "My aunt gave me a Barbie doll for Christmas once and I took it apart."

We really laughed then. And somehow it helped—Lori and I laughing together.

"But it wasn't just that. For the past few years, it's the feeling that I'm really interested in girls. That I love them, the way a guy would love them. *Anyway* . . . ," she said, and got up. She crossed the room and opened the top drawer of her dresser, then came back with a small square box. "I hope you don't mind, but I got this for you."

"What?"

"Go ahead. Open it. It doesn't mean anything."

I opened the box and found a bracelet—a silver chain bracelet, linked together with green stones.

"It's pretty, Lori," I said, holding it up.

"You said green was your favorite color."

"It is. But I didn't buy you a present."

"It doesn't matter. I'd just like to see you wear it. A friendship bracelet or something. You don't have to tell anyone who gave it to you."

"I wouldn't mind," I told her.

Lori gave me a little smile. "Well, maybe. *Anyway*," she said again, "let's see what else is on. This movie's really awful."

We had to use the bathroom downstairs before we went to bed. I went first, then Lori. When we turned out the light and got in the twin beds, I wondered for a moment if she would try to kiss me or something—whether I'd wake up in the night and find her in bed with me. But it never happened. It was just like being at Pamela's or Elizabeth's, except we didn't know each other as well. And I wondered why people seem so afraid that someone who's gay or lesbian might make a pass at them. All you have to say is no, just like you'd tell a guy who was hitting on you.

I woke first in the morning and lay with my head propped up on one hand, watching Lori sleep. I tried to imagine what it must be like to feel so different—so disconnected from everyone else. Like, what if I lived in a world where the normal thing was to like members of your own sex, and I just couldn't seem to *feel* that way about girls? No matter how I tried, they just didn't turn me on, and I kept liking boys best. And I had to keep hiding my feelings about how I felt about Patrick—couldn't hold hands with him or kiss him or anything. What if I knew that everyone expected me to fall in love with a girl and spend the rest of my life with her, and I just didn't want to?

I also began to worry that maybe Lori's giving me a bracelet meant she was about to do something desperate, the way Denise Whitlock had given me presents before she stepped in front of a train.

I tiptoed downstairs and used the bathroom, and when I dressed, I put on the bracelet.

Lori woke up when I was tying my sneakers.

"Hey, you're up!" she said. "I didn't snore, did I?"

"I wouldn't know. Slept like a log," I told her.

At breakfast, it was just Lori, her folks, and me. Her brothers were still asleep.

"What a beautiful bracelet, Alice! It matches your eyes," said her mother.

"Thanks," I said. "I like it too. I got it from a friend."

8

A Slight Misunderstanding

I decided not to say anything to Elizabeth and Pamela about Lori, because this was her own private business. I wasn't entirely sure how *I* felt about it, but Lori didn't need any more problems in her life right now. I knew I was going to talk to Dad and Lester about it, though, because I tell them everything. Well, *almost* everything.

Mrs. Haynes and Lori drove me to the Melody Inn at nine, and I was glad to see that Lori didn't appear at all suicidal. Her mom obviously loved her, and would go on loving her, even after Lori told her secret.

"Thanks for inviting me," I said as I got out.

"See you!" Lori said, and smiled.

When I walked in the Melody Inn, though, and over to the Gift Shoppe where Marilyn works, it felt as though I were walking into a morgue. Marilyn didn't say much, and her eyes got teary at the least little thing. I made it a point not to mention Lester, but that's all she wanted to talk about.

"Is he happy now, Alice?" she asked. "Is that really what he wanted—to end our relationship?"

"I don't know, Marilyn. He's just the same old Lester, I guess," I said miserably.

She turned on me then. "Well, give him a message from Good Ole Marilyn then, would you? Tell him that some day, when he's sixty years old, The Same Old Lester will be sitting in his same old chair by his same old self, and he'll suddenly wonder what happened. He'll have no hair, no teeth, no love, no joy, no woman in his life, and he'll have missed the boat completely."

"Okay," I said.

She sighed and began straightening the Beethoven mugs and the Scarlotti scarves on the shelf behind her, her long brown hair hanging loosely down her back, looking about as forlorn as she ever had. "Oh, I shouldn't be getting you mixed up in all this," she said. "But if someone were to bury Lester in an anthill up to his armpits right now, I would *laugh,* Alice! *Laugh!*"

I was glad when Dad asked me to help Janice Sherman in sheet music, but when I went over there, *she* was in a bad mood. Seems she'd heard that Miss Summers was going to England for a year, and I knew right off she'd thought maybe she'd have a chance with Dad after all. But then she'd asked him to a play at the Kennedy Center and he'd turned her down.

"Does he *really* have plans for next Saturday night, I wonder?" she mused aloud in my direction.

"Maybe he's doing something with Miss Summers," I offered, trying to be honest.

Janice dropped the glasses that hung on a chain around her neck and stared at me. "I . . . I thought she was going to England!" she said.

"She is, but they're going to write to each other," I told her, and that's when she *really* got bossy. I was glad when my three hours were up, and spent the afternoon washing all my sweaters and putting them away for the summer—getting out my shorts and sandals.

I made a chicken salad for dinner and defrosted some rolls.

"This is really good, Al!" said Dad. Then he joked, "You're going to make someone a wonderful wife."

I gave him a look, but wondered how Lori would feel if her dad said that to her.

"Thanks, but I'm feeling sort of sad for somebody," I said.

"Who? The chicken?" asked Lester.

"I'm feeling sorry for Marilyn, if you really want to know," I told him.

"Don't start," said Lester.

"I *should* be feeling sorry for you, though, because she said that when you're old and alone, sailing your boat without any teeth—"

"My boat? Teeth?"

"Well, maybe she said you'll be *missing* the boat, and when you're alone and without any love or teeth, you could be buried in an anthill up to your armpits and she'd just laugh," I finished, confused.

"I think you're both missing a few cards in your deck," said Lester, and went right on eating.

"She's crazy in love with you, and you don't even care!" I said. "If you can't love a wonderful girl like Marilyn, who *can* you love?" I sounded like somebody on a talk show.

"Would you like me to lie down on the couch, Doctor, or can you analyze me sitting up?" said Lester. "Look, kiddo. I'll tell you what I'm afraid of. I'm afraid of settling down at twenty-one with a nice girl like Marilyn and having to watch her give up her own plans in order to put me through graduate school. I'm afraid of our having a child too soon and neither one of us being able to finish college. I'm afraid of getting married so early I'll be a completely different person from who I'll be when I'm twenty-seven or twenty-eight, and that the girls I loved at twenty-one—the *girl* I loved at twenty-one—wouldn't be the same kind of girl I'd love later. And then I will have made *two* people unhappy—me and Marilyn."

"Well said, Les," Dad put in.

"And also," Lester continued, "I'm seeing another woman."

I put down my fork. "Who?"

"Her name's Eva. I'll introduce you sometime."

"Then you dropped Marilyn for Eva?"

"That was part of the reason we broke up."

I began to get the picture. Up until now, Lester had worked at Maytag every other Saturday, and done tutoring at the university. Now suddenly he'd met a woman named Eva, and had to have more money.

"Crystal and Marilyn never minded that you didn't have a lot of money," I said.

"Al, for Pete's sake, that isn't your business in the least," said Dad.

"Thank you," said Lester.

I sighed. I was still thinking of Marilyn, and wasn't sure I'd like Eva. "The world is full of unrequited love," I said finally.

"You and Patrick having problems?" Dad asked, reaching around to get the butter out of the fridge.

"No, I was just wondering what you would say if I told you I was a lesbian."

"Come again?" said Lester. "I'm having a hard time following this conversation."

Dad just looked at me. "Is this a hypothetical question?" he asked finally.

"Actually, yes, but I wanted to see your reaction," I told them.

"Well, on one level, I suppose I'd be disappointed, Al," said Dad. "On another, I think I'd be a little bit sad, and on another, I think I'd be happy for you."

"How?" I wanted to know.

"I think I'd be disappointed that you wouldn't know the happiness of having a husband and children; I'd be sad that you were part of a minority, because I know—and you know, from CRW—that minorities are usually never treated as well as everyone else; but I'd be happy if you found someone you could love. What brought this up, if I may ask?"

"I just spent the night with a lesbian," I said.

I saw Dad swallow.

"Gotcha!" I said. "You *were* worried, weren't you? Actually, nothing happened. Lori Haynes said she liked me, and she gave me a bracelet, but I told her I don't feel the same way about her, so we're just friends."

"Good for you, Al," he said. "I'm glad you're still friends."

"It's funny how people react to that," Lester said, helping himself to another roll. "Couple months ago at the U, a gay approached a friend of mine in the men's room, and my friend decked him. Now my friend's going around bragging about it."

"Why couldn't he just have said 'No, thanks'?" I asked.

"I don't know," said Lester. "It just seemed the right reaction to the proposal, he told me. To show that *he* wasn't gay. Personally, I think that a guy who has to answer a proposal with a left to the chin is protesting a little too much."

I sat there wishing that when Lori Haynes finally got up the nerve to tell her family, they'd be as kind as Dad and Lester were to me.

"I really love you guys," I said suddenly.

"That's why we know you aren't a lesbian," Lester told me. "The men in this family are so wonderful that women just have to love us most."

The following Saturday, the Saturday Janice had invited Dad to the Kennedy Center and he turned her down, he took Miss Summers to the movies instead, and I was glad, in case Janice Sherman asked me, that I'd be able to say that Dad *did* have other plans. She hadn't said anything more that morning when I'd put in my three hours at the Melody Inn, but I could tell she was thinking plenty.

It had been a beautiful April day, and that afternoon Dad had lowered the porch swing, which is the official start of spring and summer at our house. Around November he hooks it way up close to the ceiling so it won't blow around in the wind, and in April he brings it down. I washed it off and hosed the porch again. That's about as far as spring cleaning goes at our place. I did my usual Saturday scrubbing of the kitchen and bathroom (Lester does the vacuuming on Sundays), and then I started calling my friends to see what was up.

Not much, actually. Pamela had to go somewhere with her father, Elizabeth had cramps, my friends Karen and Jill were both going out for the evening, and Patrick was at a state band competition in Towson. I thought of Leslie, from school, and looked up her number, but nobody answered the phone.

About eight, I heard Lester's stereo playing, so I went up and tapped on his door.

"You're not going out with Eva?" I asked.

"I'm taking her to dinner tomorrow," he said.

"Then want to rent a movie and make popcorn?" I asked. "I'll watch anything you want—

female wrestling, westerns, sexy movies with French subtitles I'm not supposed to see until I'm eighteen . . ."

"In your dreams," said Les. But then he put down his pen and said, "Know what? I *do* need a break. You want to watch a flick, I'll rent one. Put on the popcorn."

Maybe I had mental telepathy, I thought as I melted some butter on the stove and got out the air popper. Maybe I knew what a person needed before he even opened his mouth. If that was true, I *would* make a good psychiatrist.

We only live three minutes from a video store, and Lester came back with a crime movie filled with men in dark suits, which was way down my list of favorites, but at least we were going to do something together. We sat on the couch, a big bowl of popcorn and a bottle of Sprite between us, and I'll admit I dozed off a few times. I woke the third time to see a man kissing another man on the cheek, and five minutes later, he had his head blown off.

Suddenly I had this weird thought: Maybe Lester was gay! Maybe the *real* reason he gave up two gorgeous girls and was sitting here on a Saturday night watching a movie about men kissing was that he, like Lori Haynes, was finally realizing the truth about himself. Maybe there wasn't any Eva at all. Was it possible?

I glanced sideways at Lester. He shoved another handful of popcorn into his mouth, his stockinged feet on the coffee table. To be honest, Lester had always seemed crazy for girls, but what if it was all a big put-on?

There was a car chase on the screen, and Lester's eyes were glued to the set. Both Lester and I had our shoes off, and I was barefoot, so slowly, to test him, I inched my toes toward his and sort of crawled up and down his foot. He didn't even notice! Was that significant or what?

"Man! Look at that jump!" Lester exclaimed as a man leaped from a burning building.

I gently ran my finger over his nose and upper lip.

Lester jerked around and stared at me. "Get out of here!" he said, pushing my hand away. "What are you *doing*?"

"Just a test, Lester," I said, and reached for the popcorn again.

When the movie was over, I said, "Lester, that story you told about the guy who made a pass at someone in the men's room . . . was that you?"

"What?"

"I told you you could even bring home a sexy movie with French subtitles, and instead you got a movie about men kissing."

He just kept staring at me. "That was the Mafia! The kiss of death!"

"Oh! I just thought . . . maybe the real reason you broke up with Marilyn was—"

"That I'm gay? Al, I'm in school! I've got graduate school ahead of me. I'm only twenty-one, I've met another girl, and you're insane!"

I sighed. "Okay. So I was mistaken." I didn't get up, though. "I guess I've been thinking a lot about Lori, trying to figure out just how I feel about it."

"What's to wonder about?"

"If she really is a lesbian."

"Well, I don't know, but maybe she's confused and won't know for a few years yet. She may just be going through some adolescent crushes on girls. On the other hand, if she really is lesbian, she can probably no more change than a person can force herself to like Brussels sprouts. It's just the way she is, that's all."

"Then why are there all these jokes about gays? All the teasing and stuff?"

"You tell me. Some people are just afraid of people who are different, that's all. Isn't that what CRW was all about? Prejudice?"

Lester took the Sprite bottle and bopped me lightly on the head with it a couple times. It made a hollow sound as though my head were empty.

"As for you," he said, "remember that it takes a medical degree to be a psychiatrist, Al, and you can be arrested for practicing without a license."

I had just picked up the empty popcorn bowl and was starting toward the kitchen when the doorbell rang.

"I'll get it," said Les, and I went on down the hall. I heard the door open, and then a woman's voice, followed by a sob.

Crystal!

I stood like a statue in the kitchen. Here I was supposed to be protecting him from her, and he'd walked right into a trap. How could I go out in the living room now?

"Now what's this all about?" I heard him say, but his voice was gentle.

What was she doing here? Crystal was married! I'd been a bridesmaid at her wedding only six months ago! She and Peter were supposed to live happily ever after!

"I . . . I think I made a mistake marrying Peter," she sobbed. I could hear every single word she said, mostly, I guess, because I was standing just inside the kitchen doorway.

I heard Lester close the front door and say, "You shouldn't be here, you know."

"Les, you're the only one I can talk to."

"Now that's not true."

"But I *have* to talk to you, because you're involved."

My heart almost stopped. Maybe she was pregnant! Maybe she was having Lester's baby! Maybe I was going to be an aunt!

"And how is that?" I heard Lester say.

Crystal kept on crying. "Aren't you even going to ask me to sit down?"

"Crystal, I'm supposed to be studying for a huge exam. Where's Peter?"

"H-Home."

"Does he know you came over here?"

"No. We had an argument and I went out for a walk and just walked and walked and ended up here. *Please* talk to me, Les."

"You can sit down for a few minutes, Crystal, but I'm not about to come between you and Peter."

"Why are you so *cold* to me?" she asked.

I knew I shouldn't be listening, but if I'm supposed to be helping Lester avoid her, I had to know what was going on, didn't I?

There was some murmuring I couldn't quite make out, then footsteps going into the living room. I peeked cautiously around the corner and saw that Crystal was sitting on the couch, but Lester was leaning against the living room doorway, arms folded across his chest.

"So how am I involved in this?" Lester asked.

"I think I married Peter on the rebound, Lester. I'm not sure I'm over you yet. I'm not even sure I love Peter."

The room was so quiet I could hear the clock ticking on the mantel.

"Peter loves you," Les said finally.

"I know! That's what makes it so awful. I can't stand the thought of hurting him. But, Les, I . . . I *dream* about you. *Those* kinds of dreams. I open the door, and there you are. I keep comparing Peter to you. . . ."

"It's a waste, Crystal. We had a good time together and you're a lovely woman, but I don't love you like Peter does, and it's over."

Now Crystal was really crying. "How can you be so cruel, Lester? I can't *make* myself forget, can I?"

"Maybe not, but you don't have to encourage yourself to remember, either. I think you make things seem better between us than they were. Uh . . . Crystal, excuse me a minute, will you?"

When I heard Lester's footsteps on the stairs, I knew he was headed for the bathroom. All that Sprite and no relief. . . .

I came out of the kitchen and saw Crystal getting a tissue from her pocket.

"H-Hello, Alice," she wept.

"I was in the kitchen. I couldn't help hearing," I said.

"I *love* him, Alice! It's horrible to say, but I just can't help myself," she cried.

"No, you don't," I said, and sat down beside her. I knew what I was going to say next and realized I shouldn't, but there was a marriage at stake here. "I think he's given up on women, Crystal."

"Not Lester," she said, and her nose sounded clogged.

"He practically told us so. We're trying to adjust to the new Lester. In fact, well . . . tonight Lester and I watched a video together—his choice—and . . . and it was about men kissing."

Crystal stopped blowing her nose and stared at me. *"Lester?"*

I just shrugged. Nothing I'd said was untrue, exactly.

Lester came downstairs just then.

"What's your phone number?" he asked Crystal.

She looked at him, then at me. And finally, in a small voice, she gave it to him. Lester picked up the phone in the hallway and dialed, while Crystal sat unmoving on the couch.

"Peter? This is Les McKinley. . . . Fine. How are you? . . . Listen, Crystal went for a walk tonight and ended up here. . . . Yeah, I know it's across town. I don't think she's feeling very well, and I wondered if you could come pick her up. . . . Sure. . . .Yeah, I'll tell her." Lester hung up and turned to Crystal. "He said he'll be right over, and he wants you to know he's been really worried about you."

She smiled a little. "He always worries about me." She kept staring at Lester, though. "Maybe it helped coming over here tonight," she said.

"I hope so. Because you two have a great life ahead of you, and it doesn't involve me," Lester said.

"All right. I believe you," she told him.

They talked a little about Crystal's job and how Lester's studies were going, and I stayed right there on the couch like a chaperone to see that Crystal didn't get mushy again.

Finally we heard Peter's car pull up, and Crystal went out on the porch. Lester closed the door after her and leaned against it, his eyes closed, breathing a sigh of relief.

"I can't believe I got out of that so easily," he said.

"With a little help from me," I said smugly.

Lester's eyes widened. "What did you say?"

I shrugged again. "Not much. Just that you were off women."

He scowled. "That's all?"

"I said we'd just watched a movie together . . ."

"And?"

". . . about men kissing."

"Al!"

"And that's when she decided to go back to Peter," I said. "I promised I'd get her off your back, didn't I?"

Lester looked at me in exasperation, and then he started to laugh. "I'll take all the help I can get," he said.

9

Comparing Notes

"What do you want for your birthday?" Patrick asked me the following evening when he got back from the band competition and we'd walked over to Georgia Avenue for some ice cream. And he added, "Now that you're an older woman. . . ."

Patrick likes to kid me because I'm a couple of months older than he is.

"A racehorse," I said.

"Sure."

"A driver's license."

"Keep going."

"Surprise me," I told him.

April had turned to May, and the air was sweet-smelling and soft. I realized I was probably as comfortable with Patrick as I'd ever been, but I still couldn't imagine, even in my boldest dreams, instructing him how to make love to me if we were married.

"Okay, then, what color flowers do you want for the semi-formal?" he asked.

"My dress is green. White or yellow would be nice."

"Wrist corsage or dress?"

"Wrist," I told him. I hate flowers on my dress. For one thing, I imagined Patrick and me dancing really close, me with my eyes closed, maybe, and I didn't want a bunch of flowers squashed between us.

I could tell by the way we were walking—the way he held me around the waist—that he was acting a little different that night. Clutching me a little tighter.

I was glad that the porch light was off when we got home. I'd told Dad that's one of the most embarrassing things that can happen to a girl—to come home from a date and find the porch light on. If you walk up on the porch, then, it's a signal you don't want to be kissed or, if you do want to kiss, your boyfriend has to do it with all the neighbors watching. But if you stop out on the sidewalk so he can kiss you in the shadows, it's as though you're expecting something, and what if he didn't intend to kiss you? It would be so awkward.

We sat down on the swing, and Patrick pulled me next to him and kissed me, real slow, sort of moving his mouth from side to side as though he wanted to touch every centimeter of my lips.

Then he stopped and whispered in my ear, "Tell me how you like to be kissed."

Oh, no! I thought. It was happening! I was only in eighth grade, and already a boy wanted to know how to make love to me!

"What?" I gasped.

"I just want to know how you like to be kissed. Gentle or hard or . . . there are all kinds of ways. What do you like best?"

"S-Surprise me," I said again. It's all I could think of. I didn't *want* to give directions. I didn't *want* to be the guide. I wasn't ready for this. I wanted it to be like it is in the movies, where the man knows what to do and whatever he does is just right, and the woman looks glamorous, not awkward, and . . .

Patrick turned his body toward me, braced one hand behind my back, and with his other hand pushed against my shoulder so that I was half lying on the swing and he was bending over me, kissing me hard on the mouth.

Bonga, bonga, bonga, went my heart, as a ping went through me, and at that exact moment the porch light came on.

We both tried to sit up at the same time, jerking the swing, and Patrick slid off almost onto his knees. I was grasping the back of the swing, struggling to sit up and trying to get one foot on the floor to keep the swing from coming forward again and hitting Patrick. Dad was standing there inside the screen, watching the whole fiasco.

"Oh," he said. "I thought I heard noises out here." But he didn't turn off the light. "Hello, Patrick. Would you like to come in?"

"Uh . . . no, thanks," Patrick said, scrambling back on the seat beside me where I was trying to straighten my shirt. "I guess I'd better get going. I've been gone all weekend, and I still have homework to do."

"Oh, how did the competition go?" Dad asked.

"We came in second in performance, third in sight-reading."

"Very good," said Dad. "Beautiful night, isn't it?" He went back inside, but left the front door open so that if there were any more squeaks coming from the porch swing, he'd hear them. As if we'd continue to sit out there with the light on, like we were onstage or something.

Patrick got up.

"Well, I'll see you tomorrow," he said.

"I'm sorry, Patrick," I whispered. "Good night."

As soon as I got inside, I faced Dad. "Why did you *do* that? It was so humiliating!"

"If you want to invite boyfriends to the house,

Alice, have them come inside," he said. "I don't like you sitting outdoors in the shadows."

"In the *shadows*? We were on the porch. On the swing!"

"On your back, if I saw correctly."

"You were spying on us! You were watching out the window!" I shouted.

"I just happened to glance out, that's all."

"We were just . . . just trying a different kind of kiss, and you had to turn on the light!" I yelled.

"Oh, Al," Dad said. "It starts out as a kiss, and then one thing leads to another."

"So what did you think we were going to do? Spawn or something? You sound just like Aunt Sally!" I went on.

I was starting to cry, and that really made me mad. "Weren't you ever young?" I shrieked. "Don't you remember what it was like to be on a porch with a girl?"

"I remember all too well, and that's why I turned on the light."

I knew that Dad was feeling as miserable as I was, but I didn't care. Lester walked in right then—he'd taken Eva out to dinner and come back early to study—and I realized that if Dad hadn't caught us kissing like that, Lester would have. I didn't know which would be worse. I could imagine Lester standing there watching us and saying finally, *Al, you going to come up for air?* or something.

I went right on yelling at Dad. "Is this what I have to look forward to? All through high school, whenever I go out with a guy, you're going to leave the porch light on? And if you don't leave it on, you'll *turn* it on at the most inappropriate moment?"

"Oops. I'll sit this one out," Lester said, and started up the stairs.

"If the most 'inappropriate moment' is my daughter on the swing and Patrick on top of her, then yes, that's what you can expect," Dad said.

"Whoa," said Lester, and turned back around.

"He wasn't *on* me. He was bending over me."

"That's how it all begins, kiddo," said Lester.

"Are you in on this too? Do you want me to stand here and tell Dad everything I've seen you and Marilyn do?" I cried.

"Al," said Dad, a little more gently, "it's not easy raising you all by myself, and I'm doing the best I can. A father can't help worrying about his little girl, you know."

"I'm not a little girl, Dad! I'm almost fourteen!"

"That's what I mean. That's why I worry."

"When *I* was fourteen," said Lester, "everything I saw reminded me of sex—tomatoes, knotholes, pillows, peaches, you name it."

"I don't care what you were like at fourteen,

either of you! I'm me and Patrick's Patrick and you can't tell us how we can kiss! We'll kiss any way we want!" I yelled, and stormed up to my room, banging my door so hard that I heard plaster falling inside the wall. Then I started crying and couldn't stop. It wasn't fair that I had to be the only girl in the family. What did they know about my feelings? Just because Patrick was kissing me in a new way didn't mean we were going to have sexual intercourse. If Dad only knew how embarrassing even *kissing* was for me . . . !

What was even more embarrassing was that I'd forgotten to tell him I needed a ride to school the next morning because I had to be there early. Camera Club was having a special meeting before school, and after my big door-slamming scene, I had to go back and ask a favor.

I opened my door softly and started down. I was only halfway there when I heard Lester saying, "Well, I suppose you could lock her in the basement with bread and water, but I doubt it would help. Once she's sexually active . . ."

Sexually active? Sexually *active*? Patrick and I hadn't even learned the fine points of kissing yet!

I marched on down. "For your information," I said from the doorway, as both Dad and Lester jerked to attention, "I am about as sexually active as a bag of spinach, and if you want to keep me on

the porch and not out in the park somewhere behind the bushes, you'll keep the stupid light off
when I come home with a boy."

"All right, Al. I apologize," Dad said, relief
spreading over his face. "The light stays off."

"And I need a ride tomorrow, because I have to
be at school a half hour early," I said.

"I'll run her over," said Lester. "I've got an early
class."

We sat side by side in Lester's car the next day.
The Camera Club was getting a page in the eighth-
grade Memory Book, and we were supposed to go
over the best pictures our members had taken
during the year and decide which five should go
in the book.

Lester gave a little cough, the way he does when
he's about to say something serious.

"Uh-oh," I said.

"What?"

"Here comes a lecture."

"Not really. I just wanted to say that if you knew
how much Dad worries about you—about
whether he's doing things right, I mean—you'd
go a little easier on him."

"Well, it's not exactly easy on me either, Lester.
At least you had Mom when you were growing
up."

Lester was very quiet, and then he said, "I was a couple years younger than you are now when she died."

"Oh," I said, and felt awful.

"In some ways," he said, "it couldn't have come at a worse time. I was pudgy—"

"Pudgy? You?"

"Yep. I was clumsy. It was the age when you feel that the only woman who could ever possibly love you is your mom, and then she died."

"Well, at least you didn't have to embarrass yourself in front of her," I said, and immediately knew that was wrong too. Every time I opened my mouth, I seemed to say the wrong thing.

"Not in front of her, maybe, but in front of Aunt Sally. We all lived with her and Uncle Milt and Carol for a couple of years after Mom died, you know. And if you think last night was embarrassing . . ."

"Tell me," I said, and settled happily back in the seat. If there's anything that makes you feel better about an embarrassing episode, it's hearing about someone else's that was far worse.

"Well, one day Aunt Sally caught me in the basement trying to wash my sheets."

I tried to understand. "Why was that embarrassing?"

Lester glanced over at me, then straight ahead.

"You know about nocturnal emissions, don't you?"

Good grief, what else was there to learn? I wondered. It sounded like something having to do with a car. "No," I said.

"When a guy reaches puberty and has a sexy dream he ejaculates in his sleep, and wakes up to find the sheets wet. I didn't want Sal to find out. Then she saw me."

I couldn't help smiling. "What did she say?"

Lester gave a little laugh. "'Oh.' That's what she said. I still remember. I think she was probably as embarrassed as I was. It just caught her by surprise. She said something to Dad, though, because the next day he had a little talk with me about wet dreams, just explaining it to me. That was even worse—to think they were *talking* about it, for Pete's sake."

For some reason it was pretty easy discussing stuff like this with Lester. I think it was because we were both in the car facing forward. It's sort of like talking in the dark. You don't have to look at each other.

"I have a question," I said.

"Shoot."

"When a guy ejaculates, how much semen comes out? A cup?"

"A *cup?* Ye gods, no. A tablespoon or two,

maybe." He grinned at me. "I never measured."
We laughed.

"Why do you suppose talking about sex is so
embarrassing?" I asked.

"Because it's so personal, probably."

I folded my arms and looked right at him. "So
are *you* sexually active, Lester?"

"There! Now see, that's the kind of question
everybody dreads. That's why nobody wants to
talk about sex, because they're always afraid
somebody's going to get *too* personal. And that's
pretty personal. Let's just say I get around."

"So do alley cats," I said.

"What I *mean* is . . . Well, define 'sexual.'
Intercourse is sexual, but so is kissing and hugging and caressing and sweet-talking. So are back
rubs and licking and touching and about a dozen
other things I could name. You don't have to have
intercourse to be sexual."

"Okay, okay," I said. "No more questions." And
then I added, "For now."

"Get *out* of here," Lester said, pulling up to the
school, and I grinned as I got out and shut the
door.

Patrick looked a little embarrassed when I saw
him after the Camera Club meeting, and I didn't
think that *anything* could embarrass Patrick. I felt

embarrassed all morning. Even at the meeting, I'd been thinking about Patrick, about his wanting to know how I liked my kisses, and then Sam came up behind me and said, "Which pose do you like best?"

I wheeled around and said, *"What?"* And then I saw he was holding two photos of seventh-grade girls outside the cafeteria. In one, the girls were seated, and in the other they were standing.

"A little jumpy today, are we?" he joked.

"Oh, it's just *every*thing!" I said. "I think I need a new life or a new family or . . ." I stopped, because I knew what he was thinking.

I was sure of it when he said, "Darn! Hoped you'd say boyfriend."

I just smiled and shrugged and we dropped it.

He's nice, I thought. As nice as Patrick? I didn't know.

Pamela's dad was out for the evening, and she invited Elizabeth and me over to make tacos and keep her company. We sat around the table eating supper, and I told them about my row with Dad. How Patrick and I hadn't been doing anything, really, just trying out a new way to kiss, and Lester's already talking about "sexually active."

"It sounds like I've taken up sex as a sport or something," I complained.

"Sister Madeline says that what we really have to remember is to keep both feet on the floor at all times," said Elizabeth.

"Ha! I've got news for Sister Madeline," said Pamela. "You can still get in a lot of trouble that way too. Keep both feet on the floor and your knees together! Now *that's* a challenge."

10

Sunrise...Sunset

My birthday came on a Tuesday this year. There was a huge sale going on at the Melody Inn the weekend before, and another band competition the following weekend, so neither seemed like a good time to have a party. Besides, Pamela was still moping around about her mother, and with one thing and another, no one was in a party mood.

"I don't want a party, Dad," I said. "I'm getting too old for birthday parties anyway. None of the kids I know celebrate their birthdays like that. They just hang out together or something."

"What would you like to do, then?" he asked.

"Just celebrate with you and Lester. Order in Chinese food, maybe. Patrick will probably plan something," I said.

"Whatever you want, honey," Dad said.

On the one hand, I wanted to be treated like

a grown-up. Like a cool fourteen-year-old who didn't need someone singing "Happy Birthday" for her to know she was appreciated. On the other hand, I expected everyone to remember and do *some*thing, though I wasn't sure what.

It must have been raining when I awoke on my birthday, because I seemed to have remembered the sound of rain during the night, and it was gray and depressing when I caught the bus for school, even though azaleas were in bloom all over the Washington area.

Pamela and Elizabeth remembered my birthday, of course, and brought balloons to school. Karen and Jill remembered too. We have this tradition of giving each other one of our favorite pairs of earrings on our birthdays and at Christmas—on loan, of course—and then when the next birthday comes around, we all trade again. So I got earrings from all of them.

In the cafeteria at noon, Elizabeth stuck a little candle in a chocolate chip cookie for me. Lori came by the table with Leslie and wished me happy birthday too.

"Your birthday?" asked Gwen, when she walked by and saw the candle. "Your dad taking you out on the town?"

"No, it's a busy week. We'll probably do it up big when I'm fifteen," I told her.

What really ticked me off, though, was that Patrick didn't say very much. He'd wished me a happy birthday on the bus that morning, but he didn't talk about coming over. Maybe because I didn't give him any practical suggestions about a present, he simply didn't buy me one.

"He takes you for granted, Alice," Pamela said. "He doesn't think he has to do anything special to keep you. As though he's so wonderful, you'll always be there waiting for him."

Elizabeth was more charitable. "The semi-formal's in two weeks," she said. "Maybe he's saving up for that."

"Maybe," I said. "It's not that I *need* a present—I just want him to acknowledge that today's special somehow. To make *me* feel special."

"Of course!" said Pamela.

Sam remembered, though. He's my lab partner in life science, and ever since we finished dissecting frogs, we've been grossed out examining the lung tissue of pigs. Did you know that a pig's lungs actually have dirt in them—real, black dirt? You can shake it out! The teacher went on talking about what cigarette smoke does to your lungs, and if anyone wanted to try cigarettes after that, they'd have to be crazy.

While the teacher was talking, Sam reached over and touched me. I thought he was trying to hold my hand, then realized he'd slipped a small box tied with red ribbon on my lap. I grinned at him and tried to open it without looking down so the teacher would think I was paying attention. Finally, when I felt the lid come off, I slowly lowered my eyes, and then I tried to stifle a laugh: there was a pickled frog's heart that Sam must have saved from our dissection project, and with it a note that said, *I'd give you my own, but I need it.*

The teacher turned around from the blackboard and said, "Something humorous about emphysema, Miss McKinley?"

"N-No," I stammered. "I'm sorry."

He turned to the blackboard again, and I covered my mouth as I dropped the box in my book bag. Sam and I shot smiles at each other all through class that day, and he walked me to study hall, then went on to gym.

Well, Patrick, I thought, *it's your fault. You weren't here and Sam was.*

Something dramatic—traumatic, I should say— happened that afternoon, though, that had nothing to do with my birthday. That morning, in fact, in one of the stalls in the girls' rest room, I found scrawled on the back of a cubicle door the words *Lori and Lesbo,* and I realized that somebody else knew about Lori too. I sure didn't want Lori to see it and think *I'd* written it. In fact, I didn't want anyone to see it at all, so I took my ink eraser and rubbed if off the best I could.

But it was after fifth period that I was walking by the rest room on the second floor with Pamela and heard something going on inside.

"Go on! Do it!" somebody was saying, as someone else snickered, and when I stuck my head inside, I saw that five or six girls had backed Lori and Leslie into one of the stalls and were crowding around the door.

"Go ahead, kiss her!" one of the girls laughed and, seeing me, jeered, "They were holding hands at the mall. Trisha saw them. We're just helping them out."

All the girls laughed.

"Yeah, their coming-out party," said another.

Lori's face was as red as I'd ever seen it. I didn't know that a human face could be so red. Leslie, though, looked pale, as though she might throw up.

"*Kiss* her!" another demanded, pushing Lori and Leslie toward each other, and then they all began to chant: "Kiss her, kiss her, kiss her. . . ."

"Stop it!" I stormed into the group, elbows flailing. "Just *stop* it!" I yelled. I was pushing my way in like a football player. The girls turned and looked at me, but they didn't move much. I reached out until I had hold of Lori's arm and pulled her after me, Leslie following, while the other girls jeered again.

I was angrier than I could ever remember being—far angrier than I'd been with Dad. I'd thought the kids in our school were so tolerant! I'd thought we didn't discriminate! We just had prejudice of another kind.

"Didn't CRW mean anything at all to you?" I went on. "*Listen* to you!"

Miss Summers suddenly appeared in the doorway, her eyebrows raised.

"Hey, we're not racists!" one of the girls said as I dragged Lori past her. "But we know lesbos when we see them."

"*She* must be one too!" laughed another.

"What's going on?" Miss Summers asked, coming into the room.

"Nothing," one of the girls said. Two of the others slunk away.

"A lot," I said. "A lot of ignorance is going on." I turned to Lori and Leslie. "I've got to get to class. See you . . ."

Lori was crying quietly. Miss Summers looked at me and then at her. She put one arm around Lori's shoulder, staring after the girls who were filing out of the rest room now. I went on down the hall in the other direction beside Pamela, who hadn't said a word. If any teacher in the whole school could help, it was probably Miss Summers.

Pamela looked at me when we were around the corner.

"*Are* they?" she asked.

"Who knows? What difference does it make?" I said.

She gave a little laugh. "A lot! Do you know what they're talking about, Alice? Kinky sex. Do you know what lesbians *do*?"

I turned on Pamela then. "Do you know what your mother and her NordicTrack boyfriend do? Does anyone ask *them*?"

Pamela stared at me. "Alice!"

"Well, why does everyone jump on someone who's different? If Lori and Leslie *are* lesbians, they can't help it."

"Maybe not, but they don't have to go around flaunting it."

"Flaunting it? Patrick and I can walk down the hall right here in school with our arms around each other, we can stop at my locker and kiss, and nobody says a word. But Lori and Leslie hold hands at the mall and look what happens!"

Pamela started chewing her bottom lip, which is always a sign that she's annoyed. And I thought, *Great! We're going to have a quarrel right here in the hall because I insulted her mother, and things will get worse and worse between us, and . . .*

"I didn't mean to upset you on your birthday," she said finally.

"It's all right," I murmured. "I'm sorry I said what I did about your mom." I ducked into history class, but even I knew that part of the reason I'd charged into those girls was because I was already mad at Patrick for not making more of my birthday.

He wasn't on the bus that afternoon, and I remembered he had a track meet. I slid onto a seat beside Elizabeth while Pamela hung over the back, telling Elizabeth what had happened in the girls' rest room up on second.

Elizabeth turned to me wide-eyed. "You did *what*?"

"She charged in there like a mother lion and rescued her cubs," Pamela said. "You never saw so many jaws drop."

"Well, you did the right thing, Alice, even though homosexuality *is* a sin," said Elizabeth.

"Don't get me started," I told her. "Not everyone believes the same thing about sin."

"What I mean is, *being* homosexual isn't a sin, because people can't help the way they are, but making homosexual love is."

"Isn't that sort of like telling someone it isn't a sin to be hungry, but it is if you eat?" I snapped. The Birthday Girl was getting madder by the minute. Patrick was off at a track meet, and because of that, everyone who found themselves in my way got run over.

Pamela got off the bus before we did, and Elizabeth seemed pretty glad when we came to our stop.

"Well, happy birthday anyway, Alice," she said cautiously as we separated at the corner and she crossed the street. "I hope you're doing something special tonight."

"Oh, Dad will think of something," I said, and managed a smile.

I guess Aunt Sally would say that I gave a Pity Party for myself and didn't invite anyone. I sat on the couch with a can of Pepsi, staring at the TV, and hardly even spoke to Lester when he came in. I guess the look on my face said that he'd better have a present for me or else, and he must have guessed, because he came downstairs just before dinner and set a gift on the coffee table. That's where we put presents when it's a special day, but we don't open them till everyone's there.

Dad ordered in Chinese food and let me pick the dishes, and I didn't tell them what had happened in the rest room that day because I didn't want to feel any more depressed than I was. Dad and Lester paid a lot of attention to me, of course, and when we all went into the living room to have cake and ice cream while I opened my gifts, Dad said, "I invited Sylvia to stop by for dessert, Al, but she has parent conferences tonight."

"That's okay," I said.

"Sure you don't want me to call Patrick and invite him over for some ice cream with us?"

"No," I answered. "If Patrick can't remember to do something on his own, then I'd just as soon he didn't do it at all." I knew they could hear the quaver in my voice, and I was glad they didn't say more because I might have started bawling.

I opened Lester's present first. He was grinning at me from across the room, and I could tell it was going to be something weird. It was. Out tumbled a fuzzy green octopus with big plastic eyes with black pupils. No matter how you tipped the octopus, the eyes were always pointing in your direction, so it seemed to be looking at you all the time. It was wearing a red patent-leather shoe on each tentacle and a yellow sweater with "Alice" printed on the front in pink—the craziest-looking thing I'd seen in a long time, and I had to laugh in spite of myself.

"I'll put it on top of my dresser so its legs can hang down all over the place," I told him.

Dad's present was a gift certificate for the Melody Inn, and for some reason that really upset me. What did it take to give me a gift from a store where he was manager? He didn't even take time to pick something out? He didn't even know his own daughter well enough to know what she'd like? I'll bet he even had Janice Sherman fill out the certificate herself; he hadn't even taken time to do that.

"Thanks, Dad," I said flatly. "It'll buy a lot of CDs."

But as I gathered up the wrapping paper, I could see out the window that the sun had set in a gray sky. My birthday was almost over. All I could think of was, *I'm fourteen and all Lester can give me is a stupid stuffed animal? All Dad can think of is a gift certificate from the Melody Inn? And my crumb of a boyfriend doesn't even show up? This is a birthday?*

I hung around long enough so I wouldn't seem totally thankless, and then I took my presents upstairs and sat on my bed staring down at my feet.

If I had a mother, she could do better than this, I thought, swallowing and swallowing so I wouldn't cry. About nine o'clock Dad stopped at the door of my room. I was propped up on the bed reading a magazine.

"I'm afraid this wasn't a zinger of a birthday, Al," he said. "I'm sorry we couldn't do a little more this year. Just too many things on my mind, I'm afraid."

Yeah, I wanted to say. *You're thinking more about*

Sylvia Summers leaving than the fact that I'm a whole year older. I'll be leaving home some day, and how will you feel then?

But I didn't say that. "It's all right," I lied.

He waited. "If you'd rather have a gift certificate from another store—the Gap, maybe—just tell me."

"No, it's okay. It's not you, Dad. It's Patrick. All he did was wish me a happy birthday on the bus this morning. That's it. He hasn't called, hasn't come over, no present, no card. . . ."

Dad leaned against the door frame. "Well, there could be a lot of reasons, Al. People aren't always going to do things exactly as you want them."

"But he's supposed to be my *boy*friend!" I said. "Even Sam gave me something. It was weird, but it was something." And I told him about the frog's heart and Sam's message. Dad laughed.

"Tell you what," he said. "Why don't you just sleep on it, and maybe things will look different in the morning."

"That's what I intend to do," I told him, and went into the bathroom and brushed my teeth.

I went to bed at nine-thirty. I almost never go to bed before ten—eleven, some nights. But I turned off the light and hated that I could feel tears squeezing out from between my eyelids. Maybe this was the way couples broke up. Instead of one big fight, they just started growing apart, forgetting important things. Maybe this is what happened between Pamela's mom and dad.

It's hard to sleep when you're angry and disappointed, but finally my eyelids began to feel heavy and I could sense myself drifting off.

Suddenly my eyes popped open again because there was music coming from somewhere. It sounded like a band—a band playing "Happy Birthday."

I threw back the covers and bolted up, listening, then jumped out of bed and ran to the window in my pajamas. And there on the lawn below, standing around a flashlight propped up on the grass, was Patrick's combo from school—Patrick on the snare drum, a guy with a French horn, a saxophone player, and a boy playing the clarinet.

Dad tapped on my door. "Al, I think you've got company," he called, smiling.

"I know." I laughed as he stuck his head inside. "Aren't they nuts?"

"I think they were waiting for you to turn off your light so they could serenade you," he said, and left me alone to enjoy the music. I sat on the windowsill, one leg hanging over the edge, probably the only girl in Silver Spring who had been serenaded by the eighth-grade combo on her fourteenth birthday.

I could see faces appearing at the windows next door. People came out on their porches. I felt I should be tossing rose petals down on the guys, but I just perched there on the windowsill and grinned and grinned. After the "Happy Birthday," the boys bowed and I clapped, and then they played "You're the One, Babe."

"Surprise me," I had said to Patrick, and he did.

The phone rang and Lester answered in the hall, then brought the phone into my bedroom, stopped to pick up a pillow off my bed, and delivered the phone to me on a pillow, like a servant.

"For the madam in her pajamas," he said, bowing, and I laughed.

It was Elizabeth, across the street.

"Oh, Alice!" she gasped. "It's the most romantic thing I ever saw. I'm going to hang up and call Pamela and see if she can hear the music over the phone."

When the second song ended, all four members of Patrick's combo threw chocolate kisses up at me, and I tried to catch them, and after a while there were kisses all over the floor of my bedroom. The ones I caught, I threw back and they ate them. Finally, the other boys went on home. I went downstairs and out on the porch, into the warm May night to thank Patrick. Dad left the porch light off.

It was the first time I'd ever kissed a boy in my pajamas. He backed me up against the wall and gently kissed me, a really tender kind of kiss, and I probably never felt as loving toward Patrick Long as I did right then.

I told him how much I liked his surprise— "about the best surprise I ever had," I said—and he kissed me again.

I couldn't stop grinning when I went back inside. I grinned at Dad and I grinned at Lester and I grinned all the way upstairs. Lester called, "Is the Cheshire cat happy now?"

"She's happy," I said.

But it wasn't over yet. When I got home from school on Wednesday, there was a Priority Mail package from Aunt Sally sitting between the screen and the front door. It was addressed to me.

I took it inside and opened it. There was a small gray box tied with a white satin ribbon. Inside was an old gold locket on a thin gold chain. It took several tries to pry the locket open, but when I did, I discovered a small lock of reddish blond hair. I knew right away it must be my mother's.

I stared down at the note Aunt Sally had written:

Dear Alice:

I've been waiting for the right time to send this to you. Your mother used to wear this locket as a teenager, with pictures of boyfriends inside. I snipped a lock of her hair at her funeral, and can't think of a better way to give it to you than in her very own locket. As dear as this is to me, I think it will be even more precious to you. Happy Birthday.

Lovingly, Aunt Sally and Uncle Milt

I could hardly breathe as I sat on the couch, gently stroking the shiny lock of hair that was so like the color of my own. Here was a real part of my mother—an actual piece of herself. I felt that the locket was too precious to wear. Too valuable to touch, almost. As though I should put it in a vault at the bank to protect it always.

And then I realized that this wasn't the most important part of her after all. *I* was a piece of my mother. And *this* piece should be out doing things, experiencing *life*! Exhibit A: Marie McKinley's daughter.

"Thanks for my birthday, Mother," I murmured, kissing her hair. "Thanks for bringing me into the world. I miss you. . . ."

11

The Dance

We didn't seem to be getting a lot of work done at school. They say that happens at the end of eighth grade. Most of the teachers realized that our minds were on the dance.

There were posters all over school advertising it, of course, and they made the same point: that every eighth-grader was welcome. You didn't have to be part of a couple. You could come in groups, you could come solo, it didn't matter. *Just come!* the posters said.

Elizabeth and Pamela, Karen and Jill, and I spent a whole Sunday up in Elizabeth's bedroom, trying different hairstyles and experimenting with makeup. I decided I was going to be part of the "in" group no matter how boring it was to me. Mrs. Price even said that Elizabeth could wear mascara for the dance, and with her long lashes, she looked like a movie star.

Mrs. Price also told Pamela and me that we could bring our gowns over there the night of the prom and get dressed. It was nice of her to say that, but at the same time, I felt so jealous of Elizabeth—that she had a mom to help out. I think maybe Pamela was feeling the same way. She had a mom too, except she wasn't around. Mrs. Jones was off in Las Vegas doing who knows what with her gym instructor, but I'll bet they weren't jogging on his NordicTrack.

In gym I said to Lori, "You're coming to the dance, aren't you?"

And I was really pleased when she said yes. "My dad's going to drive a bunch of us there," she answered.

"Good," I told her, and added, "I'll be wearing your bracelet. It just matches my dress."

Lori smiled back. "Good," she said.

The dance was scheduled for Friday night. When I saw Patrick in the hall that morning, he waved and smiled, but I didn't see him in the cafeteria or on the bus going home. I knew that Justin's dad, Mr. Collier, was picking up the guys first, though, then coming for the girls. We were starting out an hour early so there would be time to put on corsages and take pictures.

Frankly, I was worried about Donald Sheavers. He'd always done such stupid things when we were out in public. I didn't know why Pamela invited him to our semi-formal, except to make Brian or Mark jealous, maybe. But Donald . . . ? When I was in fourth grade, he and I used to play Tarzan together, and for years afterward, every time he saw me somewhere in public, he'd give the old Tarzan yell. It was so embarrassing.

I was too excited to eat much dinner. The dance was at eight, and they were going to have little sandwiches and things anyway, so I decided to take a shower, then carry my stuff over to Elizabeth's to dress.

"Al," Dad called, as I headed to the bathroom with my talcum and deodorant, "phone."

I picked up the phone in the upstairs hall. It was Patrick.

"Alice?" he said, and his voice sounded strange. "Listen. I am really, really sorry, but I'm sick."

I drew in my breath. "What?"

"I'm sick."

"I saw you in school this morning!"

"I know, but I didn't feel so great, and by noon I felt really awful. I've got this terrible sore throat and headache. Mom had to come get me, and drove me right to the doctor. He thinks it's mononucleosis and took some tests. If it is, it's really contagious."

"Oh, Patrick!" I said. I wish I could honestly say I felt most sorry for him, but I think I was feeling most sorry for myself. "Then . . . then we can't go to the dance?"

"Well, what I did was, I called Sam to see if he could take you. I mean, he could have the corsage I bought and everything."

"You did *what?*"

"But he's already asked someone. He's taking somebody else."

I felt as though the whole room were spinning. Patrick couldn't go, he'd actually asked Sam to take me, Sam had asked someone else when he'd already asked me first . . .

"Listen, Alice," Patrick said again, and I realized now how weak his voice sounded. He really was sick. "Dad's on the way over right now with your corsage. You go anyway and have a good time."

At least I had sense enough to say, "I'm sorry too, Patrick, and really hope you're better soon. You must be miserable. It won't be nearly as much fun without you."

After I hung up, I stood leaning against the wall, holding my stomach. I wondered if I was going to cry or throw up. I didn't do either.

Dad came halfway up the stairs. "Al?" he said. "Anything wrong?"

"What's mononucleosis?" I asked, realizing for the first time that Patrick might have something serious.

"A very contagious disease, fairly common. Who's got it? Patrick?"

"Y - Yes."

"Oh, no!"

I swallowed. "I'm going anyway."

"Good for you! That's the spirit!"

I saw Mr. Long's car pull up in front and went downstairs to meet him on the porch. He's a tall man, a lot like Patrick, only his red hair has gray at the sides.

"Patrick is so sorry," he said. "He feels awful."

"He'll get better, won't he?" I asked, and realized I had walked out on the porch in my robe.

"Oh, I'm sure of it, but it's terribly contagious at this stage. These things happen, and there's not much we can do about them, but we wish it hadn't happened right now."

"I know," I said. I thanked him for bringing the corsage. I took it back in the house, showered, put on my sweat suit, then picked up my dress and carried it across the street to Elizabeth's.

Elizabeth was holding the door open for me so I could get my dress safely inside. Pamela was already there, and they both had their makeup on already and looked gorgeously grown-up. Then they saw my face.

"What's the matter?"

"Patrick's sick. I'm going solo."

"Oh, Alice!" Elizabeth cried.

"What's wrong with him?" asked Pamela.

"Mononucleosis. It's contagious."

"The kissing disease!" Pamela said knowingly.

"What a shame, Alice!" said Elizabeth's mom. "And he'd bought your flowers and everything."

I thought of what Aunt Sally in Chicago would say if I called her: *When life hands you a lemon, make lemonade.*

"Well, I'm going anyway," I said again.

"Too bad Sam doesn't know Patrick isn't going," Pamela said. "I'll bet he'd jump at the chance to take you."

"He knows. Patrick called and asked if he could take me, but Sam had already asked someone."

"Patrick *what*? Is he crazy?" cried Pamela.

"He knows Sam likes me and thought maybe he'd take me."

"I do not understand boys!" Elizabeth declared. "He's . . . he's just encouraging the competition. What if Sam had said yes? You could fall for Sam and . . ."

"I've got to get dressed," I said, and went on upstairs with my stuff.

But the thought had crossed my mind too. Either Patrick was incredibly stupid, incredibly generous, or extraordinarily self-confident. Could I have been so generous if *I'd* been sick? Could I suggest Patrick take another girl to the dance? A girl who was crazy about him? I don't think so.

We were all dressed and combed and made up at last, and were careful not to get near Nathan, who was drooling all over the place these days because he was teething.

Pamela was striking in her purple gown with the halter top and her long dangly earrings. Elizabeth looked something like Cinderella in her pink satin dress. And I looked like somebody's bridesmaid in the jade green dress I wore for Crystal's wedding, but I didn't care, because it looked good on me. As a finishing touch, I put on the bracelet with the green stones that Lori had given me.

"That's perfect," said Pamela. "Where did you get it?"

"Lori gave it to me," I said.

There was total silence in the room.

"Lori Haynes?"

"Yes. When I stayed overnight at her house. She just wanted me to have it."

"*Al*-ice!" cried Elizabeth.

"You can't wear that, especially tonight, going solo!" Pamela said. "Everyone will think—"

"Everyone will think that it is a beautiful bracelet. Nobody will suspect anything else unless someone starts a rumor that isn't true, and if they do, I know I can count on you, as my two best friends, to set them straight," I said.

Elizabeth and Pamela immediately rallied around.

"You can count on us, we'll look after you," Elizabeth said, and like two mother hens clucking over a chick, they fluffed my hair, polished my nails, and touched up my eyeliner. Then the three of us walked across the street so that Dad and Lester could take a picture.

I slipped Patrick's corsage on my wrist, and we lined up in front of the stairs while Dad fiddled with the flash attachment. As I stood there between Elizabeth and Pamela, I thought of all the things that had gone on in this hall since we'd moved to Silver Spring three years ago. The first night, when Elizabeth and her mother had brought dinner over to welcome us to the neighborhood, and I'd been mad because Dad had promised us pizza; the time Crystal returned all the gifts Lester had given her and left them in a box at the door; all the times Patrick had kissed me here; the time I saw Dad hugging Miss Summers. . . .

Dad took a couple of pictures, then Lester came downstairs with his camera.

"Okay, ladies," he said, "say 'cheese.'" When he didn't get the smiles he wanted, he said, "Say 'cheddar.'" And when we still looked too dopey, he said, "Heck, say 'Big Mac with fries.'"

After that he stood us sideways like showgirls, one hand on the shoulder of the girl in front, the other hand holding our skirts above our knees.

"Okay, I'll pick you all up at eleven," he said, and we went back across the street. The moon was almost full, and I wondered if Patrick was looking at it, thinking about me alone at the dance.

Justin's father pulled up in front of Elizabeth's house, and both Donald and Justin came to the door at the same time carrying corsages for Pamela and Elizabeth.

I'll admit that I was astonished to see how good they looked. I'd expected it of Justin, of course— tall and blond—the handsomest guy in the whole school. But I was shocked to see how Donald Sheavers had changed. He's always been good-looking, but only a few months ago, it seemed, he was acting dumb at the mall. He politely handed the corsage to Pamela, though, and helped pin it on. He said hello to me, without the Tarzan yell, posed for pictures with Pamela, and, as we went out to the car, held the door open for us like an Air Force cadet.

I'd felt bad enough watching Donald and Justin pin their corsages on Pamela and Elizabeth, but even worse when the boys got in the backseat, with Pamela and Elizabeth on their laps, and I had to sit up front with Justin's father. I knew that if Patrick had come along, all six of us might have sat back there, all packed in together and laughing.

I felt so out of it—as though I didn't belong. Like everyone else was in, and I was out—outside looking in. *Lori must feel like this a lot,* I thought. It was the same way I felt during CRW—the way Dad probably felt when Lester and Carol were pretending to be in love and didn't let him in on the joke.

Well, I told myself as we pulled up to the school, I could either go around with a sad face all evening and be the girl everyone pitied, or I could smile and laugh and dance and compliment the other girls on their dresses.

We went up the steps together, and some of the teachers greeted us at the door to the gym. Miss Summers was there in a chocolate brown dress with gold jewelry. I would have felt better if she had invited Dad to be her escort, but she hadn't. He hadn't seemed too upset by it—it was part of her job to be there, after all, and it would be understandable if she went with Jim Sorringer, he'd told me. What gave me hope, however, was that she had invited Dad to visit her in England.

She looked surprised that I'd come without

Patrick, but I told her about the mononucleosis.

"Oh, dear," she said. "Well, you have a good time anyway, Alice. I'll bet he's thinking about you right this very minute."

The gym had been transformed into what the decorating committee called "The Gold Planet." Gold spray-painted branches were propped along the walls, gold-sprayed gravel beneath them. Hundreds of gold paper flowers hung from the ceiling, and a strobe light cast whirls of gold triangles around the gym as the band—a professional band this time—beat out a strange and haunting rhythm.

Elizabeth and Justin started dancing right away, but Pamela and Donald headed for the buffet table. Donald always heads for food. When he used to play at our house in Takoma Park, he'd gravitate toward the kitchen as soon as he got inside.

Lori and Leslie were there, but I noticed they didn't really touch. They'd dance the fast numbers together with everyone else, but as soon as the slow music came on, numbers where couples put their arms around each other, they'd leave the floor and walk around the gym talking to the other kids. I was sorry they felt they couldn't do the slow dances, but glad they'd decided to come.

"You look great, Alice," Lori said.

"So do you," I told her, and when the next number began, I got out on the floor with Lori and Leslie and a whole bunch of kids who came as singles, and we really whooped it up.

I was trying to keep an eye on Miss Summers, though, because I saw that Mr. Sorringer was there, all right, and I was trying to figure out if they'd come in the same car. About halfway through the dance, I saw her dancing with Mr. Ormand, who's married, and then with Mr. Everett, who's married too. But it was near the end of the evening that Sorringer danced with her.

What is it about your thirteenth and fourteenth years that so many things come at you at once? I wondered. I was standing over at the punch table putting some more ice in my cup and remembering all the bad stuff that had happened during the past year. Crystal left Lester, Pamela's mom left her dad, Miss Summers decided to go to England for a year, and now the dance I'd looked forward to all year found me here by myself, watching the woman my dad loves dance with another man who used to be, or still was, perhaps, her boyfriend.

As the number ended, and a slow tune began, I felt someone's hand on my waist and turned to see Sam smiling at me.

"Dance?" he said.

"Well, I . . ." I looked around to see where his date was.

"She's dancing with someone else," Sam said.

"Okay," I told him.

I put my hand on Sam's shoulder and he held me close, but not too close.

"Patrick called," he said as we moved about the floor.

"I know. He told me."

"I was really surprised when he asked me to take you. Because you know I would have taken you if . . ."

"I know," I said, remembering how he'd asked me even before Patrick did, but I was so sure Patrick would take me that I'd said no.

We talked about when the Memory Book would be out, and how we hoped we'd gotten the photos in on time to make the deadline. When the song ended, Sam leaned forward and kissed me lightly on the cheek, squeezed my hand, and led me back to the punch table again before he went off to find his date.

Pamela came over.

"My gosh, Alice, I *saw*!"

"What?"

"He *kissed* you!"

"We're really good friends," I said, but couldn't help smiling.

"*Really* good friends, I'd say." She laughed.

"Look. I like Sam a lot."

"Yeah, but—" She stopped, and I followed her eyes and saw that Mr. Sorringer was still dancing with Miss Summers as the next song began, and it seemed to me that he was trying to pull her closer. She backed away almost imperceptibly, but she was talking—talking and smiling—and then he talked and smiled back, so I couldn't tell if she backed off because she didn't want to dance close or because, at that particular moment, she just had something to say.

"Hey, Alice! Dance?"

It was Donald Sheavers this time.

"Go ahead," said Pamela. "I'm going to the rest room."

I went out on the floor with Donald and got the second surprise of the evening. He was a good dancer.

"Seems strange to see you here at our school," I told him. "What's yours like in Takoma Park?"

"Not so different," he said. "Yours is bigger, but we have a good intramural team. I play on it."

"Basketball?"

"Yeah. I'm a forward. I'm going to try out for the team in high school next year. Coach thinks I have a good chance of making it."

We were having a normal conversation! Donald

wasn't bellowing out dumb things or belching in public or scratching his armpits and making like Tarzan. It was totally amazing how much he had grown up.

In spite of the fun I was having, it seemed like too long an evening, and when eleven came, I was ready to go. If Patrick had been there, I knew I wouldn't have wanted it to end.

We went around and said good-bye to everyone. People were looking for souvenirs to take home, and then we went outside to wait for Lester. He was already there and had even put on a sport coat for the occasion.

"Ladies and gents," he said, and opened the doors of his car for us. Once again, Elizabeth and Pamela and their dates squeezed in back and, like a fifth wheel, I sat in front with Lester.

He drove each girl home first, and I noticed that he went slightly past each house before he stopped, so that we would have had to turn around to watch Justin kiss Elizabeth on her porch, or Donald kiss Pamela. Then he drove Donald over to Takoma Park and Justin back to his place.

"Good night!" I said to everyone in my fake voice, smiling my fake smile and giving my little Queen Elizabeth wave.

When Lester and I were alone in the car, I said

suddenly, "Les, drive me over to Patrick's, will you?"

"What?"

"There's something I want to do."

"He's probably asleep, Al! He's sick!"

"I know. If he is, we'll go home."

"I hope you know what you're doing."

Lester turned at the next corner instead of heading home and drove three blocks. He pulled up in front of the Longs' house. I got out and went around to the side. I knew where Patrick's bedroom was, and was delighted to see a flickering light coming from inside, so I knew he was still watching TV.

I stood there in my jade green dress, wishing I could sing. Wishing Lester had his guitar and that we could serenade Patrick, just like he'd done for me on my birthday.

Then I got this idea. I reached into my jade green evening bag and pulled out a handful of gold-sprayed gravel, my keepsake from the dance. I took a few pieces and threw them up against the shutters of his window, careful not to hit the glass.

"Al!" Lester hissed from the car.

I waited. Nothing happened. Patrick probably couldn't hear it with the TV on. He might even have fallen asleep. I threw the rest of the gravel against the shutter.

I could see a shadow moving along Patrick's wall, and then he appeared at the window. He pushed it open and leaned out.

"Alice?" he said in a loud whisper, then laughed. "What are you doing here?"

I laughed too. "I just came by to give you a souvenir from the dance. Gold gravel. You'll have to hunt for it tomorrow."

We laughed again.

"How was the dance?" I could tell from the sound of his voice that his throat was really sore.

"I wished you were there. How are you feeling?"

"Urky," he said. "Hope you didn't catch it too."

"Must be awful."

"I'll live. How was the band?"

"Not as good as your combo."

"Sure." He grinned. "You dance with anyone?"

"Everyone. There was a line clear around the gym, just waiting their turn."

"How about Sam?"

"Yeah. Him too."

"*He* was happy, I'll bet."

"Well, as I said, it wasn't you."

"I'm really sorry about tonight," Patrick told me.

"You couldn't help it."

He was quiet for a minute. "You look awfully nice."

"Thanks. Well, I should let you get back to bed. Thanks for the corsage, Patrick. It's beautiful."

"Good night, Alice. Thanks for coming by." He threw me a kiss.

I got back in the car and Lester started the engine. "Anybody ever tell you you're a nice kid?" he said. "Nutty as a fruitcake, but nice."

I laughed. "It's the least I could do for Patrick."

"Throw rocks at his window? Now that makes sense."

When we got home, I sat on the arm of the sofa and told Dad all about the dance—all except the part about Miss Summers dancing with Mr. Sorringer. Then I went out in the kitchen to put my corsage in the refrigerator.

When I opened the box it came in, I saw a small folded piece of paper I hadn't noticed earlier. I sat down at the table to read:

> *Dear Alice,*
> *I'm really, really, really sorry I can't take you to the dance. I'd like to have seen you in your green dress and danced with my arms around you. Will you take a rain check? When we're in high school, the senior prom?*
>
> *Love, Patrick*

DATE DUE

1-20-00 AV	DEC 19		
12-20-0	APR 20		
1-25-01	MAY 11		
2-24 BPS	MAY 25		
OCT 23	SEP 10		
NOV 13	OCT 1 2010		
JAN 21	MAR 12		
SEP 27			
OCT 1			
DEC 21			
OCT 11			

3961